7 Ways

Lupehole

Overcoming The Odds
Living with Lupus

Aleathea Dijon

Some names and identifying details have been changed to protect the privacy of individuals.

This book contains medical suggestions, products and natural remedies; however, no warranty is made that they will heal or cure any sickness or disease. Please consult your physician before using any of the suggestions provided in this publication. They cannot be used or in substitution for the advice of a medical professional (for instance, a qualified physician, nurse, pharmacist/chemist, and so on). The author, Aleathea Díjon is not a doctor and this is her personal story living with autoimmune diseases.

Lupehole Overcoming the Odds Living with Lupus
By Aleathea Díjon
Aleathea Díjon, LLC

www.aleatheadijon.com

Book cover designed by Styles of Thai Graphic Designs
Book edited by Concepcion Multi Services
Book formatted by B. Abby, Inferno Designz, Write on Promotions
Cover & back photos by Precious T. Photography
Edited & Foreword written by Wilson Lee Williams
Contributing title by Genard A. Williams

First Edition: February 2017
Printed in the United States of America
ISBN: 978-1542471534

a

Dedication

This is in dedication to every last one of my "Lupies". Those we lost and those still fighting this mystery of a disease. This is my experience to share with you in hopes that this may help, get you through and you may find your own "Lupehole" in life.

Acknowledgement

I thank Jehovah, GOD for allowing me to witness his works and showing me every breath you take is truly a gift, in itself.

My parents, Celeste Alexander and Wilson Williams, along with my Lisa "Ma2" Williams and Stephen "SteveO" Alexander. My very opposite sisters, Shana Rivers, for the encouragement and Javona Williams for keeping me in check. Also to my little brother and sister Kameron and Karrington in hopes you two can look up to me one day. Same thoughts for my niece, Jayda and nephews: Elijah, Ayden, and Zion. Thank you! Nakeema Collins for reminding me to keep on my spiritual armor.

A big THANKS to my girls, Brittny "YaYa" Williams, Meta Brown, Shakeena Watkins, Ebony Sowell-Franklin, Brooke Brown, Randyll Beard, Kyran Seger, Brandy Botts, and Zayna "Z" Varner for your prayers. You have been by my side literally in the hospital and making me smile. To all my extended family, thank you.

Anna, my first personal trainer, for making me sweat and keeping Lupus at the door. Juanita Ann Bates, my pain and natural healer all at the same time and Latoya Jordan, my attorney and friend.

I am so thankful for my counselor and life coach, Latasha Matthews for helping me set boundaries and holding me accountable. You have given me practical tools I can use daily.

I would like to thank the Lupus Foundation, Georgia Chapter for helping me with different resources, walking to find a cure and given me a chance to see that I am not alone.

Last, but not least, Cyrus Thornhill, my son, "my 2". You have shown me so much about life and really living. "Out of the mouth of babes" says Matthew 21:16. "A child is a wonderful reward and a reminder of the ultimate gift GOD gave."

Preface

I wanted to share my personal story about living with Lupus and how I have learned how to overcome a lot of different situations in life and how I get through. People don't discuss how you "get through". Instead they just say, "Oh, I'm praying for you" and "You can get through it" or they'll tell the end of their story and just say, "I got through." but they rarely share the details and all the in between stuff.

No matter who I come in contact with, they always ask me, "When did you find out you had Lupus and what exactly is it?" At that moment is when I feel I have to tell my story. In writing this book I had many emotions, not sure which parts of my life to share, but then I had to remember my "why". Why was I writing in the first place? I yearned to be healthy in every aspect of my life, and that entailed the word HEAL. I knew words have the POWER to heal.

Writing not only became therapeutic for me, but I had to relive some painful experiences. Although painful, I was allowing myself to be exposed on my own terms. In essence, it was my way that freed me from all the clutter in my head and the bad in my heart. To actually let a lot go and give the details of my "get through" to help another human being, especially those battling Lupus and other autoimmune diseases whether directly or indirectly was and continues to be my testimonial and purpose.

I hope to share enough details of my daily life through this tool, this method of expression that you may take your own personal life and experiences and APPLY the <u>Lupeholes</u> I found to be vital. In hopes the Lupeholes will not just serve for survival, but for you to truly live and view each breath GOD gives us as a wonderful gift. I pray you find encouragement, hope, and add your own Lupeholes to any bad contract given to you through this life and find a way out!

Foreword

Written by Wilson Lee Williams

WE ALL HAVE EITHER WALKED IN FEAR, FACED FEAR OR MAY EVENTUALLY SUCCUMB TO FEAR. Morning is defined as the period of time between midnight and noon. I also believe it's an era of one's mental process when an awakening from darkness to light occurs.

LIGHTS: A seed was planted and a child named Aleathea Díjon was born on July 13, 1985 in San Diego, California. GOD bestowed a special cherub who has been nourished and nurtured. Once a literary lamb, Aleathea Díjon has evolved full circle only to be taunted and tested. She has been stricken with a life-long disease called Lupus which prevents her from living a normal life. Aleathea Díjon is forced to focus on self and forever keep THE LIGHTS ON!

CAMERA: The Bible and its historic past have stories about courageous women and Planet Earth today mirrors and echoes the same.

This heart-compelling book entitled "Lupehole" unveils Aleathea Díjon's "Walk" down a tormented trail of "Overcoming the Odds Living with Lupus."

Her empathetic and optimistic spirit is challenged with pit stops full of pain and life-threatening obstacles are thrust to center stage.

Haven't you ever questioned GOD?Knowing Satan lives around us and sometimes dwells within our hearts; it's refreshing to know angels are amongst us as well. However, no matter how strong we may appear our souls sometime weaken to fear. What's a "safe bag" and how could the principles of the "7 Lupeholes" benefit me? "Lupehole" highlights a choice to live or lie down and allow the vultures of this disease to eat away at ones flesh and mind.

As an author, editor and publisher I understand and appreciate the impact of words specifically the realism depicting journals of journeys. Aleathea Díjon has embraced her hereditary genes of creativity and passion to educate with this and other heartfelt writings.

I'm not only a proud Dad but one of privileged ones who benefitted from her existence. I remember my daughter's birth and how it pulled me from the ashes as a troubled thug out in California to later retire as a distinguished 24-year Veteran.

I found myself immersed into factual food for thought about this disease only to have my thirst quenched from your own pouring tears.

Most can get off this rollercoaster ride once this book is put down; however the cold reality is Aleathea Díjon and others affectionately nicknamed "Lupies" must ride and live with the contents forever.

ACTION: In the end, this is a story . . . NO! NO! CUT! That sounds too trivial and mediocre. ROLL REALITY: A silly-hearted human being has been mentally, physically and emotionally drained and forges ahead for not just self but mankind as well. Aleathea Díjon transforms tragedy into tears of joy and fights every day for another breath with a GOD-given QUEST . . . to reach, touch and teach us all!

Contents

Introduction   i

Chapter 1   Why Me?   1

Chapter 2   Genre   21

Chapter 3   Safe Bag   43

Chapter 4   Knowing   61

Chapter 5   Walk   73

Chapter 6   Pills, Pills, Pills   91

Chapter 7   Orange is NOT the new Black   103

Chapter 8   Fear of Forgiveness   128

Chapter 9   At Last   136

Chapter 10   Autopilot   145

Endnotes   160

Glossary   161

Resources   176

Introduction

What is a Lupehole?

According to Merriam-Webster, a loophole is an opening to admit light and air to permit observation. It is also, a means of an escape or an ambiguity or omission in the text through which the intent of a statue, contract, or obligation may be evaded. Some synonyms for loophole are alternative, escape clause, outlet, technicality, and simply put, a way out.

Loophole, commonly used in law and "getting out" of contracts, I needed a Lupehole to get me out of Lupus. In trying to find one, I found seven. And I continue to find more. Let me share the seven Lupeholes that I have discovered while overcoming the odds, living with Lupus and just daily life's obstacles!

Everyone wanted me to categorize my book. I say it's neither here or there. It's not totally a self-help book because I am still learning to help me, but in turn I truly hope it helps at least one person.

It's not a medical book because I am not licensed, nor do I have a degree in the medical field. I don't think medical coding & billing counts; however it is my own personal experience with life and in how I have learned how to cope with daily life and it's anxieties on top of dealing with and combating Lupus, amongst four other autoimmune diseases. I hope to share my personal story to help someone, bring awareness, and to let you know you are not alone to those that have been diagnosed with Lupus or if you know a person that is affected by this mysterious disease.

We are, in all the same, living here on this earth, and we all have been dealt cards. I figured if this is the hand I have been dealt, I'm a pretty good spades player, I am going to get at least one book.

Did you sign your contract on life?

Are you looking for a Lupehole to get you out of that bad contract to a fresh start?

Do you feel that you didn't sign up for some of the hardships in your life? Let's get you out of them.

There is a Lupehole to every law, rule and statistic, but I have found SEVEN.

Let's find your Lupehole!

Lupehole

Lupehole

The Lupus Foundation of America estimates that 1.5 American suffer from Lupus, and at least 5 million people worldwide have a form of Lupus.

Why Me?

I reached for my cell phone under my cold pillow and turned off the alarm. I squint and adjust my vision. It was Dr. Lowinski, my primary care physician calling. Oh how I hoped to sleep in because it was Friday, November 11th, 2011. Not only was it my day off and Veterans Day, but my now infamous 11/11/11.

"Good Morning, are you able to come into my office so we can discuss your results?" Dr. Lowinski, asked. As soon as she asked, I knew in my head the results were not good. I figured, if the outcome is good they usually just tell you over the phone, or not call at all.

"Yes, I can be there in 30 minutes," I answered.

Even though I felt it in my heart that the results were positive, I stayed optimistic and hopeful. So, my husband and I got dressed and headed up to Northridge Family Practice Medical Center. We arrive and we sat down. The wait seemed to be hours. It's always so cold and dreary in doctor's offices and from the wait I began to worry as a lump sat in my chest. I could barely swallow, then finally my name was called. We got escorted and directed to have a seat in a small examining room; time decided to just continue to drag. Dr. Lowinski finally comes in with a blank grimace and it was difficult to read her thoughts from her face.

She spoke, "I want to discuss your test results. I know we told you it may be just a rash or bed bugs over the last few months, but, we tested your blood for Lupus as you requested and your results came back positive, ANA, speckled pattern."

I knew to ask only after Lexi told me this is exactly what I had, her mother also had Lupus.

At this point I heard her, but I blanked out. Everything got real cloudy. My body was physically in the room, but my mind relocated itself to the ocean. That's where I find most peace. Like when you put a sea shell up to your ear to hear the ocean. We all know that it's a myth, it's the surrounding environment sound, but we do it anyway. Instead of crashing waves against the rocks, I heard Dr. Lowinski as, "Did you hear me? Can you hear me?

Dr. Lowinski was right in my face, but I had faded away.

I responded, "Yes, yes, are you sure?"

Dr. Lowinski answered, "We'll we ran your blood work three times, meaning that you in fact have Lupus, that is what it's more commonly known as, but the more specific type you have is Systemic Lupus

Erythematosus or SLE.   We triple checked, I assure you.

"Assure," not really the word I wanted to hear, but here I was sitting there with the medical expert who knew more than me on the subject. I sat there knowing I had no other choice, but to listen.

Also, your EKG came back showing sinus tachycardia, meaning you have an elevated heart rate, Dr. Lowinski added.

I took a deep breath and turned on Positive Patty and said, "Okay Doc, what we need to do?   As if she had just told me the best news ever.

"What we need to do first, is schedule you to see a specialist, a rheumatologist.   You need to see the specialist quickly! I want you to see Dr. Devy; he has been doing this a very long time."

We made the appointment right then and there so there was no delay, but since I had an HMO I had to wait a few days for the referral authorization to be accepted. I scribbled my Daily Scriptures calendar for November 16, 2011 to see Dr. Devy.

Leaving the doctor's office, I called the person who delivered me.
"Hey Mom, I just left the doctor and they said I have Lupus" I informed.

My Mom responded, "Okay, hmmm, wow, I'm going to call you back, I am in the middle of coordinating a wedding, but we will beat it, okay? Okay? Okay. I will call you back.

I thought, a wedding, not knowing at the time, but the bride to be, would turn out to be very significant in my life, a health guru.

Wednesday seemed to have dragged on forever, but just like the sun rises, it came. I decided to see Dr. Devy during my lunch break alone so "Lupus" wouldn't inconvenience my time or anyone else's. I get to his office and it looked just how I felt, old and grungy. I sat down and thought this man doesn't know what he is doing. It seemed as if I was his only patient waiting. The receptionist had noticed my face and yells over to me, "I've been working with him for over 35 years!"

I was relieved and then an elderly little lady scooted by me from the patient room, looked at me and said, "He'll get you back working', Tin Man."

It was somewhat eerie, but then a mild, calm voice called my name and I found myself to the room.

He introduces himself, "I am Dr. Devy and I'll get you back moving again."

Dr. Devy didn't ask me one a single question. He comes over and begins examining me.

"Ah huh, ah huh," he repeated every few seconds.

From my scalp to the soles of my feet Dr. Devy mentally takes notes of his assessment of me. He takes his stethoscope out and while examining me, shrieks back and then steps out of the room with the door slightly left open. I noticed Dr. Devy making a call; he had to leave the room because it wasn't cordless. Dr. Devy was definitely an ol' school physician. I realized he was calling my primary doctor and I'm definitely eavesdropping. I had the right; it's my life they were discussing.

Then I hear Dr. Devy say, "She's going to need another EKG immediately! Can she have this done at your office? Next thing I know, he is yelling at her, "This is absurd!"

Dr. Devy slams his fist down several times upset. "What kind of primary doctor doesn't have a working EKG system in their office?! She needs this test done right away, this is urgent!

At that moment my chest began to hurt with sharp pains. I desperately began to gasp for air, tears sprinted to my feet, and my body became spaghetti. The end result, Dr. Devy found me on his cold floor. It seemed I couldn't go anywhere else, but to the mercy of this cold floor.

Dr. Devy comes back into the room to find me overwhelmed with emotion on the floor. He helps me up. I was 26 years old at the time and all I could remember asking him was, "Am I going to die?

"You're going to be just fine child." Dr. Devy answered with a crisp sincerity, but I looked up at him with uncertainty. At that moment in time, I sadly realized I was no longer Superwoman. It felt like someone had stolen my cape. I knew it was a disease, but I didn't know how serious it was. We left the small exam room and went into Dr. Devy's office. I slowly looked around very intrigued with all his medical books and degrees. He explained that Lupus is life-threatening. This meant a whole different lifestyle, a whole different mentality, a whole different me.

The easiest way Dr. Devy could explain it to me was my immune system becomes hyperactive and attacks itself, including good tissue and organs. It's an autoimmune disease where it cannot differentiate between healthy and foreign substances so it attacks at any given moment and anything it wants. It's systemic, which means all systems, from the nervous system to the lymphatic system, the cardiovascular to the respiratory system. With all Dr. Devy's education and knowledge I still wanted him to say there was a chance the diagnosis was a mistake.

Dr. Devy further explained there is not one particular test to take, but 11 criteria that **The American College of Rheumatology (ACR)** established in 1982. It was later revised in 1997 as a classificatory instrument to operationalize the definition of SLE in clinical trials:

SEROSITIS: PLEURITIS (INFLAMMATION OF THE MEMBRANE AROUND THE LUNGS) OR PERICARDITIS (INFLAMMATION OF THE MEMBRANE AROUND THE HEART); SENSITIVITY = 56%; SPECIFICITY = 86% (PLEURAL IS MORE SENSITIVE; CARDIAC IS MORE SPECIFIC).

ORAL ULCERS (INCLUDES ORAL OR NASOPHARYNGEAL ULCERS).

ARTHRITIS: NON-EROSIVE ARTHRITIS OF TWO OR MORE PERIPHERAL JOINTS, WITH TENDERNESS, SWELLING, OR EFFUSION; SENSITIVITY = 86%; SPECIFICITY = 37%.

PHOTOSENSITIVITY (EXPOSURE TO ULTRAVIOLET LIGHT CAUSES SKIN RASH, OR OTHER SYMPTOMS OF SLE FLARE UPS); SENSITIVITY = 43%; SPECIFICITY = 96%.

BLOOD—HEMATOLOGIC DISORDER—HEMOLYTIC ANEMIA (LOW RED BLOOD CELL COUNT) OR LEUKOPENIA (WHITE BLOOD CELL COUNT <4000/μL), >LYMPHOPENIA (<1500/μL) SENSITIVITY = 59%

RENAL DISORDER: MORE THAN 0.5G PER DAY PROTEIN IN URINE OR CELLULAR CASTS SEEN IN URINE UNDER A MICROSCOPE; SENSITIVITY = 51%; SPECIFICITY = 94%.

ANTINUCLEAR ANTIBODY TEST POSITIVE; SENSITIVITY = 99%; SPECIFICITY = 49%.

IMMUNOLOGIC DISORDER: POSITIVE ANTI-SMITH, ANTI-DS DNA, ANTIPHOSPHOLIPID ANTIBODY, AND/OR FALSE POSITIVE SEROLOGICAL TEST FOR SYPHILIS; SENSITIVITY = 85%; SPECIFICITY = 93%. PRESENCE OF ANTI-SS DNA IN 70% OF CASES (THOUGH ALSO POSITIVE WITH

RHEUMATIC DISEASE AND HEALTHY PERSONS)

NEUROLOGIC DISORDER: SEIZURES OR PSYCHOSIS; SENSITIVITY = 20%; SPECIFICITY = 98%.

MALAR RASH (RASH ON CHEEKS); SENSITIVITY = 57%; SPECIFICITY = 96%.

DISCOID RASH (RED, SCALY PATCHES ON SKIN THAT CAUSE SCARRING); SENSITIVITY = 18%; SPECIFICITY = 99%.

The criteria were not intended to be used to diagnose individuals and do not do well in that capacity.

*For the purpose of identifying patients for clinical studies, a person has SLE if any four out of 11 symptoms are present simultaneously or serially on two separate occasions.

I looked over the list and I accepted the diagnosis. Not realizing I had ten out of the 11 SOAP BRIAN MD criteria. Dr. Devy hands me a list of over ten medications I needed to pick up that night. I read through them one-by-one. I noticed some of the medication; I needed to take several in one day. I skimmed over Dr. Devy's "chicken scratch" writing and this is what was deciphered:

Plaquenil 4x/day (200mg) Inflammation

Prednisone 2x/day (20mg/15mg) Immune System

Sucralfate 2x/day (1GM) Ulcers

*Meloxicam 1x/day (15mg) Joint Swelling/
Muscle Stiffness*

*Tramadol 4x/day (50mg) Mild Pain (if it doesn't help
STOP by Dr. Devy)*

*Folic Acid 1x/day (400mcg) Cardiovascular and
reproductive health*

Ferrous Sulfate 1x/day (325mg) Red Blood Cell Formation

*Tylenol Arthritis 4x/day (650mg) Pain/
Fever Reducer*

Zantac 1x @ bedtime (150mg) Heartburn

Omeprazole 1x before eating (20mg) Acid Reflux

Sunscreen SPF 50 Skin Protection

At a glance with some quick math, I figured I would be taking over 20 pills a day. Realistically, I could be taking a pill every hour of a day, plus.

"Will I have to take all this for the rest of my life?" I asked.

"It's part of your management care plan. Some you will while others you won't. Some you are only taking because of drug interaction and side effects." Dr. Devy explained.

I sat still trying to take it all in as Dr. Devy continued.

"In the meantime, I need you to visit Cardiology Care to see a cardiologist for some testing and I also need you to go get some blood work from Quest Diagnostics. One more thing, "I also need you to go see this other specialist at Thurman Pain Management to help with your pain. They will provide you with a much better pain management plan."

"I will take care of this tomorrow because I need to get back to work." I commented.

Dr. Devy gave me a fatherly, stern glare and said, "YOU need to let your job know you will be in tomorrow, all of this needs to be completed today."

The smoke was clearing and the light bulb finally came on. I now had seen why people stuck with Dr. Devy for years. I left his office, a little more confident, but still in shock, thinking "why me?"

I managed to call Tax Resolution Services with a shaky voice, "Hey Lorina. Can you let my team know I won't be able to make it back into the office? I have to go get some more testing done today.

"Okay. Are you alright?" Lorina responded and asked.

"I hope so." I answered.

"No problem Chica! Will do! See you tomorrow." Lorina relayed before she hung up the phone.

Being my little organized self, I made a plan and was determined to get all my testing done. I located the cardiologist. Apparently, it's the most important because it involved my heart. Unfortunately the office was the furthest from the other facilities.

Finally, I arrive at the cardiologist, and the entire time I'm thinking "heart attacks, heart disease .... I'm like eighty years old." I get changed for the tech and I begin to ask a lot of questions. He replies, "I am not qualified to tell you exactly what's going on but I can answer basic questions. What I can tell you is that you're here for Lupus. Most of the time, Lupus patients have what's called pericarditis. This may be why your specialist ordered this testing."

With another thing added to the list, I couldn't think. I needed to go get the other tests done before closing times.

I leave the cardiologist, get in the car, drive away and approach a red light. I grab my phone and Google "pericatitis." Did you mean: *pericarditis?* Ugggh, but thanks Google."....inflammation of the lining around the heart." Wow, no wonder why my chest is always hurting. A quick light change and I run over to Quest Diagnostics next for my blood work.

Now mind you, I've always had issues getting blood drawn. I have small movable veins as the nurses say. I have veins that collapse and disappear like a magic trick, and for this reason, my son believes I'm an alien. Dehydration can also play a major part in a good stick. It took four people to draw 20 tubes, the amount of blood that they needed to run the CBC panel for different tests.

11

After all the exhaustion of being poked and probed, I had a good feeling to go see someone who specializes in pain and managing it.

The pain management specialist was right around the corner. We discussed my pain level and the best prescriptions to take. He explained to me there will always be pain; the medications just mask it and alleviate you from feeling the pain sometimes. The pain management specialist also suggested I get a pet, a dog perhaps. Getting a dog would keep me moving and serve as companionship.

Now, remember when I said I organized my appointments to get them all done? I had all this down pat. I knew exactly every location I needed to go to, the route to take to get it all accomplished. That's what I do! Give me a task and I'll get it done.

I have come to the conclusion lists are great, however if you stick to them too much, you forget the small things in life that are also just as important. I forgot the common day necessities, though small, they actually matter.

I'm leaving my last appointment and my "Silver Bullet" that would be my automobile disturbingly notified me she needed gas. Oh, that bright, orange light flashed on illuminating another tasks as if I didn't already do enough in one day. I hoped, prayed and cruised slow that I could make it to a gas station. I arrive at the gas station and there are chains around all of the pumps, but one. The doors are locked and my debit card seemed to have been in my other purse. Great, my purse was at home.

Ladies, "Why do we switch out our purses so much?"

Guys, "there is no need to chime in on this one."

All I had was cash. I walked up to the gas station store to see if the attendant would take my cash so I can use the one pump that had freedom. He answered, "No, the machines are down. Try AM/PM."

"Ok, thanks," I said, but was really thinking no thanks.

I was hungry and became very fatigued, another symptom that comes along with Lupus. It's like pregnancy exhaustion, but five times worse. I thought I can get to the next gas station so I began to cruise at 20 mph. At this point, I didn't care who was behind me. I merely waived them to go around. I'm driving down Saticoy Street and suddenly, my car clunks out! Just stops! No chugging or warning of any sort. I grab my cell phone to call my husband and to my surprise my phone is completely dead. I was so worried about all the testing, I didn't put gas in my car, nor did I charge my cell phone. With a dead car and phone, death crept into my mind.

There I sat in my car for a minute, just thinking what to do. I knew I needed a phone. It was getting dark now, so I looked for a house with lights, then a house with either women or children. I get out of the car and I walked turtle-style, my joints were on fire. Slow was the way to go. Now I understood why older people moved slowly. Slow eases the pain. I approached a house with a family, but I didn't see any women. I was cautious, but I needed a phone and

13

quick. I get to a house with an opened door with a screen. I knocked and kind of looked around nervously. Suddenly a man came to the door.

"I'm sorry to bother you. My car broke down and I ran out of gas. I need to call my husband," I informed.

"Okay, I will bring the phone outside for you," the man replied.
He returns with the phone and hands it to me. I dial my husband.

"Hey, I ran out of gas. I need you to come get me or bring me some gas," I said.

"Okay, where are you? Where are you calling me from?" He questioned.

"I am on Saticoy between Reseda and White Oak. My cell died," I quickly answered.

"Why would you let this happen? Were you not thinking? Uggh. I'm on my way," he blurted out before hanging up. Click.

I thought, no are you okay, no care at all.

I know the man heard him. Holding tears back, with the feeling of disappointment, I handed the man his phone back with a fake smile.

"Thank you, he'll be here shortly," I said in a painful, lonely voice.

14

I walk back and I'm just sitting there in my Toyota Solara coupe on the side of the road. Waiting, waiting, and waiting drove me to a deep sense of depression. I completely fell apart, I break down. All the way down as I begin hitting the steering wheel. Crying and emphatically yelling, "WHY ME?" WHY ME, WHY ME GOD! Crying uncontrollably, exhausted, hungry, feeling all alone; so, so alone. Full of emptiness is the feeling I felt as I sat there. I was helpless and hopeless all at the same time. I couldn't even speak as my lips just quivered. From my nostrils snot ran freely past my chin. I realized while sobbing the whole day I've been doing everything alone. I moved, decided, drove, and thought without GOD. Thinking I can get everything done on my own, never once did I consult HIM. As I sat there in this little cramped car all I could do now is cry, balling myself up into fetal position in the driver seat. A position we all know too well. I felt like a baby, when it's in their mother's womb or comforting arms. I cried out to Jehovah in prayer:

My Heavenly Father, I'm late, but I ask for your guidance, and I know people say don't question you, but you invite us to ask. Matthew 7:7 says "Keep on asking, and it will be given YOU; keep on seeking, and YOU will find; keep on knocking, and it will be opened to YOU. I'm asking why, why me, why did this happen to me? Why do I have to suffer? Why do I have to have this pain?

Then I began to scream at him in frustration and anguish.

I lamented at him, *"am I not a good wife GOD, am I not a good mother, am I not a good servant of you GOD, am I*

15

not a good daughter, or a good friend. I try my very best and this is what I end up with? Thank you, thank you!!!

I sensed a lot of time passed since I last spoke with my husband; however, I had no way of telling the time. So I tried to stay patient.

I began to pray again and I asked GOD with a whisper, why me one last time. Now I was calm, I began to have one of the most intense, most meaningful conversations with GOD I had ever had. Approaching HIM again with a different mind frame that day, I didn't feel like a step daughter, or abandoned, or like HE caused this to happen to me. No, I felt as though I belonged to HIM and that HE would take care of me, **as long as I relied on HIM.** That was one of the most honest and intimate prayers I've ever had and felt GOD's love and protection. I felt closer to GOD, as if I crawled up to him and he held me in HIS bosom.

I whimpered a little more and fell asleep, feeling safe, right on the side of the road.

Bang! Bang! Bang!
I was awakened abruptly by a Hispanic man banging on my driver side window. Talking fast and saying some words in English.

"Why are you here? You park in my way! Move! Move! Move! My family will be home soon and no one will be able to get in," the Hispanic man urged.

When I awoke I had forgotten all about the Silver Bullet's thirst. I didn't realize that I had ran out of gas right in front of his driveway, and at the time only appeared to be a wall.

I spoke to him through the window and said, "Please understand, I've had a really rough day."

I'm explaining to him my whole entire day is if he really knew me or if he cared. "I went to this doctor and that doctor and that specialist and I ran out of gas, I ran out of gas" poured out in a troubled voice. With tears in my eyes and said again. "I ran out of gas."

"Okay, okay! You wait! The Hispanic man responded.

I became a little terrified, like where was he going and what is he about to do?

He comes back from his truck.

"You wait. I have gas for you. My family will be home. We have to move you." The Hispanic man slides his gate open and disappears.

I got back out of the car and walked to the same house to make another call. The man appears and once again brings the phone to me. The phone rings.

"Hey, are you close?" I ask my husband.

"I've been circling around, where are you?" he asks in frustration.

"I am on Saticoy, between Reseda and White Oak. You can't miss me."

17

"Oh, okay, okay. I was on Saticoy between Balboa and White Oak."

"Okay, just get here, please, it's getting late, I desperately pleaded before hanging up.

I headed back to my car and thought to myself, I don't think he understands the pain that I am in.

I see the Hispanic man comes from his garage and comes back with a red gas can.

"There's only a little, I use it for the lawn, but it may get you to the gas station."

The Hispanic man pushes my car out of the way of the entrance to his house while he commands me to push the accelerator. I follow his direction.

"You are good now! Buenos noches mi hija. Good night."

"Thank you, thank you! I said exhaustingly, but grateful. The Hispanic man called me daughter and I smiled with gratitude.

My husband finally shows up with our son, Cyrus in the car, both well-dressed. With everything going on that day, I forgot that it was Wednesday, Bible Study.
"We'll the man that lives here, put a little gas in. I think I can make it now, but just to the gas station." I spoke with confidence.

"Okay, I will follow you there." My husband replied.

We arrive at the Texaco, which was walking distance to the Sorrento, our place.

"Are you going to Bible Study?" my husband asked.

"No!" I snapped.
"I'm too tired," I added as my rage mounted.

Then with a calmer voice, I uttered, "I had a long day and I need to go to Rite-Aid to pick up this list of medications. You guys go ahead. Tell everyone I said, Hello."

We went our separate ways. Not only was I tired, but hurt on how he treated me and the situation.

I get to the pharmacy and it took a while to fill all my prescriptions. I didn't realize I hadn't eaten all day. I bought snacks and walked around waiting for the pharmacy technician to call me and explain the proper instructions and timing for the medications. This was a lot!

I could have left my car in that parking lot that night. Living in Los Angeles you always have to parallel park on the street somewhere. That night it seemed to take forever to get a spot to park. I was frustrated. I would have walked home, but my pain level decided for me. I just wanted to get home. I just wanted to take a shower and sleep.

Finally I reached my apartment door, walked to the bathroom to take a shower, but didn't make it.

We all have the "*Why Me?*" moments in our lives and continue to try to find the answer. The answer is not revealed to us until we are ready to accept the answer.

I cried myself to sleep, right there. Right there on the bathroom floor.

Self-Notes

We all have asked ourselves this at one point in our life and we may in the future. What is your "Why Me?" Write in the space below, by the end of this book, my hope for you, is that you get your answer:

_____

_____

_____

_____

_____

_____

_____

_____

_____

_____

_____

_____

_____

_____

_____

_____

African Americans have 3-4 fold increased risk to develop Lupus than any other race.

Genre

I couldn't let this "Lupus thing" distract me. I was still breathing and looked at that as another opportunity to live, to dream and accomplish SOME thing. I tried my best to continue life as normal as possible. There was a shadow of sadness over me and I needed to shake it. So, I dove into songwriting. It was medicine and I wrote and massaged my songs while at work. I always had a passion for writing. It began as a poetic form, but then I began to hear melody behind my words. I didn't want to look like I was defeated, even though I felt that way daily. I didn't want to be this death sentence that had been given so prematurely. I wanted to switch my focus on something that I loved and enjoyed. So that's what I did. I talked to any and everybody about songwriting. It was something I could get excited about. It was truly something to look forward to.

Every function they had regarding songwriting in Los Angeles, I was there. I joined some organizations, just to stay abreast. One organization in particular was the National Association of Record Industry Professionals (NARIP). I met the President, Tess Taylor. She was more than encouraging. When people say "no," just look at it as a "not yet," she would say and she let me share my story at a few events. Ms. Taylor encouraged me to be around songwriting and other writers and even to be a fly on the wall as an observer in writing sessions. She stressed to absorb the art of songwriting. I had already written many songs, but I needed to work on my craft and to really embody it in my own way, through my own experiences.

At this point, I was excited, but still exhausted. I was dealing with fatigue, still working, being a wife and mother. The joint pain only seemed to have worsened. So I pushed myself more trying to prove to myself that Lupus would not interfere with my life, with my living. I decided to enroll at The Songwriting School of Los Angeles in Burbank, California.

This was an amazing time for me and a learning experience. I met some awesome people who were like-minded, that I still talk to this day. It's always good to be around people with similar viewpoints, but I realized this is where iron sharpens iron. This is where Proverbs 27:17 came in. Even though you may think you are good at something, you can always learn from someone else, get sharper from constructive criticism, and grow from others. So I needed to see where I stood. I wanted to know if I really had what it took.

I was so nervous my first assignment to write a verse and a hook. So I took the simple approach in my eyes. I did what I know, and that's R&B, Rhythm and Blues.

So this was not your normal classroom setting. I mean they had instruments and studio rooms. Here, you just don't just hand in an assignment like a traditional school. The teacher was none other than the multi-platinum music producer and songwriter, Mr. Erik "Blu2th" Griggs.

Mr. Griggs asks, "Who would like to go first?"

So eager I was, just to get it over with, I shot my hand up. I begin to read the lyrics, and he says, "No, noooo! You got to sang it, in here!"

I then was put on the spot for real.

I say, "Mr. Griggs may I close my eyes or turn away?"

I wanted to be a songwriter but behind the scenes. This center stage with onlookers was not my format. Unsure of myself I quickly went into my shell and got a lump in my throat. I realized everyone was waiting on me. So I had to force myself now, to really get done with it. In front of the entire class:

"Uh mmm," clearing my throat. "This song I wrote is called:

"We Don't Really Need"

Verse 1
We don't need any music
Cuz I'm gonna sing to you
And no need for them candles
Baby, I'm enough light for you
I ain't slippin' in to any lingerie
I'm so soft, baby I can't wait
But don't you worry babe

Hook
Cuz we don't really need, we don't really need
Nothing but each other
We don't really need, we don't really need
Nothing but our love
So Baby, please let's start our pleasure!

I looked back at my classmates and they weren't saying anything. Doubt quickly filled my body. I thought maybe my song wasn't good enough, but I was happy and relieved. It felt great I pushed myself, got over a fear and went for it.

Then one of my classmates Zee spoke.

"Wait you wrote that annnd you can sing?" Zee exclaimed by singing his sentence. "That was some sexy R&B. The melody was dope!

I felt elated by Zee's feedback and then a few other classmates commented and shared the same sentiment. Some even asked for my number to collaborate later.

This was my first Lupehole.

Lupehole #1: Music

This Lupehole was finding my voice and my artistry without digging too deep into other's opinions, because an opinion is just that, an opinion. A view or judgment formed about something, not necessarily based on fact or knowledge.

It felt amazing to share something I created and worked on behind closed doors. This something was a part of me, and for others to get it, to understand and appreciate my love for music. I shared a piece of me, but I didn't feel like I just gave it away with nothing in return. I was filled with gratitude.

"Music gives a soul to the universe, wings to the mind, flight to the imagination and life to everything." – Plato

Late that night after class, my classmates and I hung around talking and trading ideas. Suddenly, the teacher looked at me and asked, "Can you sing your song again?

Mr. Griggs began to play the melody on the piano.

Do you play any instruments? He also asked.

"I mean I play a little guitar." I answered.

I had been getting private lessons from Roland, my coworker on many lunch breaks. He advised I learn some chords on a piano, it fit me better. I told him I had a thang for country and it was something special to me about a black girl with a guitar.

Mr. Griggs continued playing my melody again on the piano and asked me to sing along. Now, I was comfortable and everybody else started singing the hook.

I then said, "Let's just do the entire song." And we did:

Verse 2
No need to take a fancy trip, I'm right here
No need to do no naughty dance
Baby just look, baby just stare
No need for an aphrodisiac, Baby just relax
And don't you worry Babe

Hook
Cuz we don't really need, we don't really need
Nothing but each other
We don't really need, we don't really need
Nothing but our love
So Baby, Baby, please let's start our pleasure!

Bridge
No flickerin' flames
No incense burnin' no smooth grooves low
No champagne, Babe
Cuz I am in full control
Just you and I
So let's get it started tonight!

I wrote this song for couples. I wanted to show them you don't need all that "stuff," but just each other. The deeper message was that couples would prevail with love for one another, and everything will be alright.

"Since you want to be a songwriter, you have to shop your songs. Do you have an artist in mind you would like to sing this?

"Yes" I responded and then it got a little personal.

"I want to give this song to Toni Braxton," I eluded while trying to hold back my tears.

Everyone agreed she's amazing, but they didn't understand the connection and why I became so emotional.

I didn't really tell too many people what was going on with me, but later that night I felt compelled. It was the first time I told people other than my family and friends about my diagnosis. I told them I had recently been diagnosed with Lupus and I just wanted to live and do things that made me happy. Furthermore, life is short and you have to actively live your dream no matter what the dream is, it's what keeps us alive, hope. Then they understood, because Toni Braxton was also diagnosed with Lupus prior to me.

They all encouraged me and thought it was a great idea to reach out to Toni Braxton and her team. Not even realizing the time, it was, almost midnight and I had to get home, time does really fly when you're having fun and your entrenched in your passion.

I finally get home and had to get serious with myself. I noticed on all the medications, one in particular, prednisone, kept me wound up and wouldn't let me sleep. Prednisone is a synthetic corticosteroid drug and is used to treat inflammatory diseases, but its side effects were the worse. Insomnia, depression, weight gain, especially in the face, which is often called "moon face," my friend Brandy told me I looked like I had cheek implants. When I took a closer look at my face, I realized Brandy was right. I felt like someone had injected cement in my face and it was super heavy.

So I took advantage of the insomnia, since I was up I tried to use the time wisely. I began researching and finding every possible lead to get me to Toni Braxton's team, from her label to her management.

Some time elapsed before I started to build relationships with many people in the music industry in LA. After emails and phone calls, I had to thank social media. A management company appeared on something she liked. It was an urban/pop department so I researched the company and found who was an affiliate, Mr. Marquise B. Grant, I found him!

I told myself all I needed to do is get my song over to Mr. Grant and he would be able to help me. Now back in the day, it wasn't this easy to send a record over and get back a nay or yay, so this became challenging, but I had a little help. Eventually I had to look up his information on . . . yep, you guessed it! Facebook! Back and forth I went in trying to decide whether to send him a friend request. I mean this guy doesn't know me. What should I do? Either he is going to accept it or not. As I'm pacing back and forth, jumping up and down, I hit the friend request button, and literally run. There I was glancing at the computer to see if he will accept my friend request. I found myself frantically pacing back and forth, again and again.

Even though it was what I wanted to do, I still questioned myself, what did I just do? Moments went by and I thought to myself he is going to accept it because we had many mutual friends. So with growing confidence, I walked away from the computer. I look back and have an email from December, 29th 2011 (12/29/11), Marquise B. Grant confirmed you as a Facebook Friend. I was ecstatic! Confirmation, exhilaration, jubilation…everything filled me but wait. Okay, but what do I do now? So because it was around the holiday, I waited. I wasn't sure what to say, so on January, 4th, 2012 (1/04/12) I sent Mr. Grant this message:

Dijon Pen   9:37am Jan 4

I don't know how this works as I am new
to the music industry. I have written over
100 songs and want to get them placed.
In particular I have one song that I would
love Toni Braxton to do. I am just taking
my chances and asking….please help if
you can or where to start.

Thanks so much!!!

Later that morning, Mr. Grant responds, "Send the record to: with his email address."

Now I knew my record was in no shape or fashion complete, but I had to go with what I had. I sent over a very raw version of the song and the all the lyrics. Then it was a waiting game.

I was nervous once again, but I was proud of myself for getting the resources, finding out the "who and how", and ultimately getting in contact directly. I felt triumphant in just that. BOOM!

In the email I left my contact information. I figured he would reach out to me if interested and I left it at that.

A few days later I get a call from an LA number, thinking nothing about it. It was Mr. Grant. Acting nonchalantly, but trying to hold my scream inside.

"Hi Mr. Grant." I greeted.

"I love the lyrics. I see where you are trying to go with this, but it needs more work. You got something. Get it demoed out and make it come to life. One more thing . . . never send your complete lyrics, just a taste. So keep going, but we will not be accepting this placement at this time."

"Thank you so much Mr. Grant, I really appreciate your feedback! I said gratefully and excitedly.

I went back to work letting all my coworkers know, yeah, I spoke to someone heavy in the music industry. He said I have potential. Although, it was good to hear, I knew I needed to do a lot more.

I still attended many songwriting functions, boot camps, and writing sessions. It was definitely not over for me because when you love something, it just doesn't go away in one night or after one no. I had to remember a no is really just a not yet.

I realized some things cannot be learned or given, but experienced. I was experiencing music. All these people around me believed in me, but I didn't reach the point of believing in myself. I had to reach out to someone that was like a second mother to me on the West Coast, Miss Carole Brown.

While all my family was on the other side of the country in Atlanta, and my Dad traveling all over in the Navy, I needed something that felt like family. Miss Brown took me in like a daughter and pampered my need for family. I met her through one of my best friends in high school, Meta Brown, my one year and six days a part sister. It was her Aunty Coupe, which later became my term of endearment to her as well. I was glad she moved to LA and I could reach out to her.

Little did I know she lived 15 minutes from me and her Dad, Pops lived seven minutes from me. I started to feel like I had family close by. I began to spend a lot of time with them. Parties, showcases, store runs, whatever and of course music ran all through their family. Everyone who has ever been around the Brown Family, knows the feeling, they take you in as family.

During this time when I wanted to get into music and knew I could count on her to point me in the right direction. Without a doubt Miss Brown could show me the real deal of the music industry. I would show her my songs and sing to her becoming more confident. Miss Brown managed artists and helped them develop

stage presence. She introduced me to many other
people behind the scenes.

One, in particular, I became very fond of was
Mercedes Layne. We just clicked and an instant
friendship through music developed. Not only did
music become a Lupehole to Lupus, but from my failing
marriage. I needed an outlet, a way out. So I could say
I'm going to do something with music and felt free to
leave the house with no questions asked. Music was
more than a hobby; it gave me a feeling of
empowerment and escape.

It was a matter of time before I had to express to
Aunty Coupe what I was really dealing with at home, my
diagnosis, and how depression crept in. I had a lot of
really missing my family in Atlanta and feeling alone.
She reassured me I was family and they were all there
for me. The Brown family are a very open family when
someone was in pain, it was almost as if they took it on
as well. One of her nephews, Lil' Tommy became like a
knight in shining armor for me. I've known him since
high school.

Lil' Tommy always came to my rescue in my time
of need like a brother. I tried to not "bother" anyone
with my issues, because I knew everyone was dealing
with their own stuff. Somehow I was able to open up
to both Mercedes Layne and Lil' Tommy who passed
no judgment. Another nephew, Jerrod had found out
about my diagnosis and excitedly told me to call Dr.
Sebi, he can cure anything! They kept me in good
positive vibes. When things got a little crazy they all
had my back. They consistently reminded me to focus
on my health.

I had an upcoming doctor visit with Dr. Devy to see how I was doing and to discuss my lab results. Dr. Devy looked pale examining me and I looked him in his eyes.

"Dr. Devy, how are YOU doing? I genuinely asked.

To break the silence, he just replied, "Old."

We laughed.

My lab results were serious, so Dr. Devy got right to it. He said, "We have already gotten through a lot, but there is more, lots more, but you are a tough cookie."

He explained to me that because I was on such a high dosage of prednisone, 65 milligrams it caused my glucose levels to increase. This put me at risk for diabetes. I was now dealing with pre diabetes. Pre diabetes meant that my blood sugar level was higher than normal, but not yet high enough to be classified as Type 2 Diabetes. My blood levels were all over the place.

My anemia had worsened; it was the culprit of making me feel tired and weak. Even if all I took was two steps, I was out of breath. Anemia affects about half of all people with active Lupus and I was no exception. My hemoglobin, the protein inside the red blood cells (RBC's or erythrocytes) was not carrying enough oxygen from my lungs to all the tissues in my body, causing a decrease in my RBC production. I was prescribed a slow release iron 75mg, twice a day for the iron-deficiency and more pills. Hmmm, the pharmaceutical companies were raking it all in.

I also developed what is called pre-leukopenia. My white blood cells or leukocytes had decreased significantly, which are a highly important part of the body's defense against infections. So I became more prone to infections, weakening my immune system even more, with added time to heal on its own.

Basically, if this could be basic, my body was a warzone and no one knew what side they we're on. No allies, everything was an enemy killing off their own kind. So now adding two blood disorders to list, what else could there be. The medications seemed to cause more damage than healing.

Regardless the futile playing field and bad hand dealt, yes he continued reloading with more negatives.

"When you have one autoimmune disease, you are more susceptible to others. Your results showed you also have Rheumatoid Arthritis, and Osteoarthritis, which confirms why so much joint pain and that feeling you describe as a chill to your bone. You'll need to also go see an Ophthalmologist, your results also showed you have Sjögren's Syndrome, but they have a few more specific tests they need to take."

I interrupted Dr. Devy and blurted out, "What the hell?!!"

My body immediately tensed up and I dropped my head into my shoulders sitting on the examination table.

My eyes were like a broken dam as the floodgates became overwhelmed with uncontrollable tears.

"You're kidding me, right?"

"No, I am not. Your other results with the chest x-ray came back. You have Pericarditis and Pleuritis."

"I looked that one up, but what is Pleuritis?" I asked.

"Pleurisy is inflammation in your lungs lining, that's what also is contributing to your chest pain and your shortness of breath," Dr. Devy explained.

"No offense, Dr. Devy," dragging my words slowly, "I can't take anymore today."

Knowing exhaustion was one of my biggest symptoms, it was understandable.

Dr. Devy told me, "You are 26 years old." You're young. You can fight!"

I complained of a snake skin like rash developed on my back which was painful and difficult to move. Dr. Devy determined it was from the Meloxicam I had been taking and removed that from my Rx list. He prescribed more meds to pick up and also scheduled another appointment in two weeks.

I am usually strong but had to admit I couldn't handle all this being thrown at me, what felt like at once. I buckled down and reached out to Dr. Sebi. I called and waited what seemed like days before I had gotten a response. I understood Dr. Sebi was a busy man, but I felt I was dying. As the phone was answered, a caring voice arrives on the other end.

"Good afternoon." Dr. Sebi greeted.

"Hi Dr. Sebi" and my rambling followed. I thought he could give me everything in one phone call, and looking back, Dr. Sebi did just that. I wanted answers about my health, but he asked me, "What are you afraid of?"

He was worried about my mental state.

I answered his question with, "I am afraid to die."

Dr. Sebi then went on to say, "eat from the earth, eat, what GOD has already given us."

While on his website, all I could think was "his products are too expensive." He then assured me that everything was from the earth and to be careful what I was fueling my body with. I cherished that ten minute conversation and I had to pull myself together.

Again, I used my car not only to get from A to B, but as my personal sanctuary. Right there in the parking lot, I got in my ride and the water works began even more. I could have cried the Nile River. I was tired of crying.

Before entering the house, it no longer felt like a home. I sat there a little longer, talked to Jehovah before writing a song about what people go through and still smile. I entitled it, "Private War." You never know what a person is going though. These few lyrics helped me to be more compassionate towards other humans; significant and heartfelt words on paper.

Through all what felt like daggers being thrown at me, I felt strong and decided to unwind. My first Lupehole of Music had me put on my Anita Baker, my Frank Sinatra, my Sade, and whoever else spoke to my soul. Even Jazz filled my ear ways. I had a glass of wine and soaked in Epsom Salt. Once again music soothed me, got me out of my day and out of the feeling of hopelessness.

Now Music may not be your thing, but what this Lupehole showed me was I can always go to this place to find an escape through my passion. No matter if I was writing lyrics, or listening to vocals or instrumentals.

The art of music, the beauty and harmony of it can be a very powerful Lupehole to uplift your spirits, make you laugh, and bring back good memories. It brings peace and unites people. Music can definitely heal in my eyes. Music can affect the body in many health-promoting ways and serves as the basis for a growing field known as music therapy. You can get therapy in a lot of ways.

According to the American Music Therapy Association, music therapy is the clinical and evidence-based use of music interventions to accomplish individualized goals within a therapeutic relationship. It can address physical, emotional, cognitive, and social needs of individuals.

Even if you're not able to see a credentialed professional you can however use music in your daily life and achieve many stress relief benefits on your own.

Music Therapy by Daily Activities

- *Getting ready in the morning*
- *During a commute*
- *Cooking*
- *While eating*
- *Cleaning*
- *When paying bills*
- *Working out*
- *Before bed*

Music has the ability to spark a memory or even enhance your current mood. I know if I am sad or depressed, I need to put my Adele away. It would also help me sleep depending on the undertones of the music, which consist of binaural beats or isochronic tones as they are called, like a heartbeat or rain.

Being aware of your emotional state and adding the right soundtrack can be used as a daily Lupehole.

Learn your passions, embrace them and allow them to be a Lupehole to get you out of struggle, pain, or any negative feeling or space. Pour your heart into it. Your art is you, let yourself shine and know we have been given the tools to get through.

We constantly yearn for peace, so if you ever hear me humming a song of any genre, I just might be going through a storm, and that's my peace, my calm, a Lupehole to get me through.

Self-Notes

How can you use Music as a Lupehole?

_____

_____
_____
_____
_____
_____
_____
_____
_____
_____
_____
_____
_____
_____
_____
_____
_____
_____
_____
_____
_____
_____
_____
_____
_____
___

Safe Bag

I didn't want to break the egg shells, so I walked lightly. Not saying too much, staying in my own bubble. I would get to our studio apartment still clothed from work and begin cooking without a word. Afraid I may say the wrong thing, or set him off. Dealing with an illness and not a happy marriage, I couldn't possible imagine what would happen next. While on short-term disability from my job, I received a letter from the company which employed me. Mind you, when I started with this company it only had 20 employees that number had grown to over 200. The letter stated I was being laid off, let go, terminated. I felt I contributed a lot to the growth of the company and felt betrayed with no heads up, no warning, anything. This was a major setback since I provided the only income for our family at the time. My stress levels went up, I got even sicker and I needed help. I was tired of holding the weight on my own and I needed to be humble.

I typed a letter to my landlord and explained:

"Unfortunately I have been on disability leave and I was laid off. I have decided to return to Atlanta, where my family is because I needed the help and support."

In actuality that was true, but now I couldn't even pay the rent that was approaching in two weeks. I knew I would forfeit my deposit for not paying February's rent, but I didn't care, I just wanted out. I had been a good tenant from the previous 11 months and I gave the proper notice. The Landlord was gracious and allowed me to stay with no additional burden, but I needed to figure it all out.

The end of the month approached like lightening quick and it was time to depart the premises. I packed all my belongings in pain and sweat. You could say I was sick as a dog, with flu-like symptoms. Many people explain Lupus like that. If you know how the flu feels, but all the time, that's Lupus. I removed the food from the pantry and refrigerator and handed it out. I gave away furniture, even electronics. I was getting rid of everything for I wanted nothing. I was done knowing to take just the essentials. My neighbors began to notice and tried to help.

"How could a man sit back and watch his sick wife move everything?" one neighbor commented.

I couldn't' tell you, someone that can't even pretend to care. My husband towered over me like a child as if I was taking his toys his mom bought for him.

"You can take that. No that's mine." My husband childishly spoke, forgetting I had his child.

Without communication I told him to fend for himself, not letting him know where we were going. Me, Cyrus and Smoke, my blue-nosed Pit bull puppy, grey coat, blue eyes. I took the advice from my pain management specialist to get a dog. I remember when I drove two hours away to pick Smoke up off a Craigslist ad. He was a vibrant dog. His energy helped me get out and walk. Yes, Smoke turned out to be a good companion. He knew when I didn't feel well. I recall pruning Smoke into becoming my service dog. Eventually I was going to sign him up for an accredited service dog training program. Unfortunately that was short-lived. I miss Smoke.

I finally packed my car to the roof that night. Cyrus and I slept on the floor, while he my caring husband lied in the bed. I left everything else behind. There was only room for me to drive, Cyrus without a car seat holding Smoke and his dog food. I didn't have a plan, but pulling out of the apartment gate, I bent the corner by the Rite-Aid, where I would pick up my medications and I prayed. I needed to pause and let my body catch up to my mind. I was restless. I sat there for a minute and knew I needed to get a roof over our heads, a motel, a hotel, something. How with no money, no credit card, and no one had any idea what I was going through, what would I do?

For the most part I was ashamed. I didn't want anyone to know I allowed such ill-treatment from my "so-called" husband and been putting on a good mask, the fake face of a good wife. Cyrus was four years old, but he knew what was going on. I refused to stay at a shelter, but it was an option until I could get our plane tickets. At that moment I realized I needed to find a new home for Smoke. I couldn't take care of us and worry about a dog. A friendly man walking a dog passed by and I yelled over to him.

"Hey! You want a dog?"

"Sure!" the man excitedly responded.

I explained to the man where Smoke got his shots, gave him his food and toys, no charge. "I just can't take him where we were going." I sadly uttered.

The man accepted him with excitement, expressing he wanted a second pet.

I drove off and Cyrus began to cry.

"You gave Smoke away, you gave Smoke away!" Cyrus repeated with tears pouring down his face.

At that point, I began to cry and pulled over. I had to pull myself together and explained to my son.

"We have to go; it's just you and I, Cy and I, ok? We will be okay. Mommy has to find somewhere for us to sleep." I told.

I drove around all night. I parked in front of a friend's house, but never went in. I just felt safe to sleep there for a while. I got up with my eyes batting to find the local county office.

I was the first one there, just sitting in the parking lot waiting for it to open. Cyrus was still sleep. I worried about getting us a place and food. The county office finally opened and without an appointment I was able to be seen right away being the first one there. I explained my situation, but I had to wait there all day. There was nothing else I could do, but wait with Cyrus

45

until I got what we needed. Finally at around 3pm they called me to a back room to sign paperwork. They gave me enough funds to get a hotel for a week and for basic essentials, they provided EBT including hot food, for restaurants because they knew I would be in a hotel not being able to cook.

I was thankful, humble, and grateful. GOD always provides and I experienced humility. We ALL need someone, if that wasn't the case, you would be on your own planet . . . alone.

I checked into the hotel, with a hot shower and a nice meal. Cyrus and I slept like babies. I wasn't able to get our plane tickets until another week after our check out. I got them for February 12, 2012 (2/12/2012). I still needed to figure out one more week.

I called Aunty Coupe and forced myself to give the details of my ordeal. I'm moving back to Atlanta to be with my family. I'm in a hotel right now, but our flight doesn't leave until another week.

Without another word, she said, "you and Cy take the girl's room."

Once again, just grateful, knowing that GOD places people in your life at the right moment.

I arrive at her house and it smelled like home. She was always cooking for the soul, just what I needed.

She asked me, "Do you have everything you need. Before I could answer she started listing items.

"Oh no! I don't have his birth certificate." I answered. Then I remembered I still had my safe bag.

In the midst of a crumbling marriage and on so many medications, I sought out an African American, male, therapist, intentionally. We will call him Dr. Savin. I thought he could give me the inside on what I was dealing with.

Instead of focusing on my husband, he focused on me, my health and most importantly my sanity. Dr. Savin was surprised I wasn't having a nervous breakdown. He was just a little bit late. Six months before I was found outside in my robe with nothing underneath looking for a cat I didn't own. I was going out of my mind and I knew I desperately needed professional help. Dr. Savin decided to put me on depression and anxiety medication. Great, more pills.

I was going through a cycle. One, I didn't know how to stop or how to get out. I received notice the state along with Los Angeles County Child Services had me under investigation. Little did I know, a neighbor overheard our domestic dispute one evening and made a phone call to the authorities. I explained to my therapist I need to get out, but how, they are trying to take my son. It was now necessary for me to move, but I had no family and no one to help. The same day I received the notice from the County for a social worker visit, I moved out of our one bedroom into my studio. I hired "help" and in less than five hours I was gone.

Dr. Savin gave me the tools to trust in GOD and have wisdom.

"Make sure to always have a safe bag," Dr. Savin instructed.

He handed me a list. I took it nervously, thinking I will never need this.

Eventually, we were trying to work things out, how convenient he was put out his place where I had left him. Wanting my marriage, I allowed him back. The physical abuse had ceased, but the verbal continued, the treatment was hit or miss.

Despite wanting a broken marriage to work, I realized it was not going to fix itself. I had had enough. So one night I packed Cyrus and me, along with our "safe bag" as Dr. Savin called it and urged me to have. I didn't know what to do, but I wanted to be prepared. Generally, a safety plan, with a list of items packed while if afraid in your home or combating with yourself to leave an unsafe and/or violent relationship.

At 2am, I tiptoed out the front door to my Silver Bullet. I struggled to put this safe plan in my trunk, where you keep the spare. My husband would never look there, I thought. I took the duffle bag to the car and prayed out loud at the wee hours of the night, "Please GOD I hope I never need to use this."

If you are in an abusive relationship, think about...

• Having important phone numbers nearby for you and your children. Numbers to have are the police, hotlines, friends and the local shelter.

- Friends or neighbors you could tell about the abuse. Ask them to call the police if they hear angry or violent noises. If you have children, teach them how to dial 911. Make up a code word that you can use when you need help.
- How to get out of your home safely. Practice ways to get out.
- Safer places in your home where there are exits and no weapons. If you feel abuse is going to happen try to get your abuser to one of these safer places.
- Any weapons in the house. Think about ways that you could get them out of the house.
- Even if you do not plan to leave, think of where you could go. Think of how you might leave. Try doing things that get you out of the house - taking out the trash, walking the pet or going to the store. Put together a bag of things you use every day (see the checklist below). Hide it where it is easy for you to get.
- Going over your safety plan often.

If you consider leaving your abuser, think about...

- Four places you could go if you leave your home.
- People who might help you if you left. Think about people who will keep a bag for you. Think about people who might lend you money. Make plans for your pets.
- Keeping change for phone calls or getting a cell phone.
- Opening a bank account or getting a credit card in your name.

- How you might leave. Try doing things that get you out of the house - taking out the trash, walking the family pet, or going to the store. Practice how you would leave.

- How you could take your children with you safely. There are times when taking your children with you may put all of your lives in danger. You need to protect yourself to be able to protect your children.

- Putting together a bag of things you use every day. Hide it where it is easy for you to get.

ITEMS TO TAKE, IF POSSIBLE...

Children (if it is safe)
Money
Keys to car, house, work
Extra clothes
Medicine
Important papers for you and your children
Birth certificates
Social security cards
School and medical records
Bankbooks, credit cards
Driver's license
Car registration
Welfare identification
Passports, green cards, work permits
Lease/rental agreement
    Mortgage payment book, unpaid bills
    Insurance papers
    PPO, divorce papers, custody orders
    Address book
    Pictures, jewelry, things that mean a lot to you
    Items for your children (toys, blankets, etc.)

Think about reviewing your safety plan often.

In 1984, just a year before I was born *"staff at the Domestic Abuse Intervention Project (DAIP) began developing curricula for groups for men who batter and victims of domestic violence."*

I was intrigued how visually I was able to use some of their tools to see how different types of abuse were affecting me.

Power & Control Wheel

The Power and Control (Violence) Wheel is a way of looking at the behaviors abusers use to get and keep control in their relationships. Battering is a choice. It is used to gain power and control over another person. Physical abuse is only one part of a system of abusive behaviors.
Abuse is never a one-time event.

This chart uses the wheel to show the relationship of physical abuse to other forms of abuse. Each part shows a way to control or gain power.

*Note - For more information please visit the resource section.

I was so glad I packed my safe bag and I really needed it. It put my mind back four years ago when Cy at just three days old and I had to get on an airplane. Yep! You read right, three days old.

The police told me the night before when Cy was 2 days old, they could take my child from me and place

Aleathea Díjon

DOMESTIC ABUSE INTERVENTION PROJECT
202 East Superior Street
Duluth, Minnesota 55802
218-722-2781
www.duluth-model.org

him in to custody with the state of California, if I were to go back home.

My Dad didn't ask me what I wanted, but advised me to get on the plane with my mother or else....

Some education about being in an abusive relationship that involves children whether one parent is not violent is to understand the state could intervene and show negligence on their part for remaining in the environment or household, with the abuser. Remember there is more than one type of abuse, not just physical. The truth is NO type of abuse is okay. It is said verbal abuse is actually more damaging because it hurts you mentally and much more difficult to forgive. A black eye can be hidden and then healed. That mark can be forgotten because it's out of sight and out of mind thus enables you to move on.

I do not agree with the old adage "Sticks and stones may break my bones, but words will never hurt me."

I agree more with Robert Fulghums' sentiments which state:

"Sticks and stones may break our bones, but words will break our hearts".

I had to go and felt I made the best decision for my life and my son's. It wasn't running away, but running to something better.

I remember the day I left, the day before February 11, 2012 (2/11/12), tragically that was the day Whitney Houston passed away. I called my best friend, Meta.

"Are you okay?" I asked.

Meta was heading to LA, and I was heading out for ATL. It hurt me knowing I couldn't be there to comfort her, but I was praying. Even though this shocked the world, I was hurting for her and the rest of the Brown/Houston family. It was her aunt, Tia, as she called her. I had slept in her home, and enjoyed other moments with her, I couldn't believe it. I learned something very valuable in that season of my life after her funeral.

This was what I felt all along in my life. It was the feeling of inadequacy and not being good enough. When Kevin Costner spoke at Whitney Houston's funeral, he shared she didn't feel good enough, even though she was the essence of beauty and renowned as "THE VOICE." It resonated with me and during that time I found my second Lupehole.

Lupehole #2: Self-Worth

Self-worth or self-esteem is the sense of one's own value or worth as a person; self-respect.

Self-worth in my eyes cannot be taught because it's not an external force or feeling. Others can help you to see it, but you have to feel it for yourself. It's definitely internal. You have to constantly work on it. Like a heartbeat rhythm, up and down, constantly checking in with oneself; for it is vital. If not, having low self-esteem can lead to your physical decline. It all adds up in such a negative way.

In 2016, the American Heart Association at glance states cardiovascular disease is the leading global cause of death, accounting for more than 17.3 million deaths per year!

So many people may ask ones, "Why are you on drugs? Why are you allowing yourself to being abused? Why are you broke?"

The answers are not so simple to say. We as people tend to not know what self-worth really means; nor where to start or how to find it. The lack of self-esteem and respect for one's life comes from being damaged outwardly and then harboring those feelings inwardly.

When you are damaged, just like a product, you get thrown in the unwanted bin. Here one is labeled in the no longer useful pile and eventually thrown away. You feel WORTHLESS.

It may be harsh, but it's reality. We all need not tough love, but genuine love for self. If you love yourself enough, you do not tolerate certain behaviors, attitudes, or spirits in your life.

I can recall different times in my life I would say, "Whatever I do, it's just not good enough. I'm not good enough. I'm just average and mediocre."

I remember other times I didn't even want to look at me in the mirror. My reflection was not even worthy. I didn't see what everyone else saw, but only how I felt. All in which were negative lies that I began to feel as true. Once again I found myself signing a contract I didn't have to sign.

I couldn't even imagine one of the most beautiful, talented, down to earth women would ever feel she wasn't good enough. The song Whitney Houston sang, "Greatest Love of All," written by Linda Creed and Michael Masser, didn't hit me until Mrs. Sylvia Johnson, my son's great grandmother broke it all the way down for me.

"….*I decided long ago, never to walk in anyone's shadows*
If I fail, if I succeed
At least I'll live as I believe
No matter what they take from me
They can't take away my dignity
Because the greatest love of all
Is happening to me
I found the greatest love of all
Inside of me
The greatest love of all
Is easy to achieve
Learning to love yourself
It is the greatest love of all…"

This was the love you have for yourself.

Remembering she was also human and many of us share that same feeling, we have to learn how to combat those feelings of inadequacy. We can replace those feelings with deep hearted affirmations.

It was difficult to look at that mirror and say to myself, "YOU are beautiful" every day, but every day it got easier, and I began to believe it!

"To fall in love with <u>yourself</u> is the first secret to happiness."
– Robert Morely

We all allow outside factors, sometimes to dictate our worth and search for validation from others except from ourselves or even the one that created us.

The scripture at Genesis 1:26 states:

"and GOD went on to say: Let us make man in our image, according to our likeness..."

And at Psalm 139:13-14:

"For you produced my kidneys; you kept me screened off in my mother's womb. I praise you because in an awe-inspiring way I am wonderfully made. Your works are wonderful, I know this very well.

If we look to Our Creator, HE knows us best. Just like an architect that designs a home. HE knows its blueprint, its functions, its flaws, and the best parts to show off. Most importantly it displays a reflection of HIMSELF as the creator.

I've learned through these simple scriptures perfection is not key for we will not be able to obtain it right now, but knowing who created you is.

Jehovah says I am wonderfully made and in his image.

Wow! How amazing to understand that, grow from and begin the journey of finding your own self-worth.

Once you capture your self-worth, DO NOT allow circumstances, feelings, or any outside factors to change how you feel about yourself.

So I had to leave and get on that flight back to those that I knew really loved me and supported me.

Self-Notes

How can finding and keeping your self-worth be used as a Lupehole?

_____

_____

_____

_____

_____

_____

_____

_____

_____

_____

_____

_____

_____

_____

_____

_____

_____

_____

_____

_____

_____

_____

The most common cause of death in people with lupus is kidney failure and heart related issues.

Knowing

I boarded my flight back to Atlanta and sat next to, two teenage boys. Usually I'm a talker, but I had a lot on my mind. I just wanted to remain silent, but of course they spark up a conversation with me. I was becoming more comfortable to talk about my Lupus and when they asked why I was moving back to Atlanta, I was very candid. I told them I had just been diagnosed with an autoimmune disease, Lupus and I needed my family. Both of their mouths dropped, in a way with excitement. They had shared with me that when they were much younger their mother had been diagnosed with Lupus, SLE, same as me.

Since I was recently diagnosed they told me they were sorry and knew how hard life would be for me in the future. They were so cute! Much younger than me, but had so much advice to give. "Take your medicine, ask your doctors a lot of questions, take notes because you will forget, and most importantly surround yourself with love. We love our Mom so much and love her so much more because she pushes through the pain." On that flight was the first time I heard that. Push through the pain. I think GOD was looking out for me, letting me know I wasn't alone and many different people suffer from Lupus. Caucasians tend to deal with more skin related issues, whereas African Americans tend to have more organ involvement, another odd I had to learn how to cope with.

I finally land and it felt like so many burdens were lifted. I could breathe for a second. What a wonderful feeling to just sit and observe others at the airport. I took time out to witness loved ones running towards each other, smiling, hugging, kissing and helping with bags. I couldn't wait to see my family for the sake of something familiar and something safe. I arrive at my Mom's house and just felt mixed emotions. I was first exhausted, excited and depressed, all at the same time.

Here I am separated from my husband, with a life threatening illness, living back with my Mom trying to combat the feelings of becoming a statistic with the idea of becoming a single Mom. I just wanted to shower and sleep. When I went to take a shower, my Mom had a large mirror in her bathroom, large enough so you can see every angle of your body before getting into the shower. I didn't really look at myself much. I had gained over 60 pounds on prednisone, more weight than in my pregnancy. I could barely lift my leg to get in the shower and the joint pain was excruciating. I remembered what the boys on the airplane had said though. I had to push through the pain. Little did I know at the time, but Lupus began to attack my nervous system. As soon as I got in the tub, I had an ugly slip and fall. I sat there in tears, still questioning "Why me?" I realized it would be difficult for me to stand for long periods of time, so I really needed to be mindful of that, but then my memory played tricks on me too, 'til this day. I would forget to take my medicine, to eat, or even to sleep. I had to learn how to nap while everyone else was busy. I felt like a waste of a human at that point. I loved being busy and independent. I had to learn how to not only depend on others, but trust others.

Not even days later I developed a high grade fever, which landed me back in the ER. The ER staff took very good care of me and prescribed more medicine, including something for my falls and dizzy spells. The ER doctor also recommended one of the best rheumatologists in the area and I had to follow up with her in three days. She leans in and says, "She's amazing! Just so you know she's an African American." Her statement only meant she would be more understanding and relatable.

I finally had my office visit and waited so long I wanted to leave. Then I met the rheumatologist and I must admit she was on 10. Her energy was amazing, she was amazing!

I asked the rheumatologist, "Not to be rude, but why is the wait so long?"

She replied, "I love taking care of people's health. It means their life, so I go over everything before someone leaves my office. So let's get started."

With her explanation and caring demeanor, I felt like the wait was worth it. I mean she was really there for me and wanted me healthy. The rheumatologist and I went over a new plan, a better plan. She told me I needed to walk, to add supplements, and try and talk to someone because managing Lupus is very difficult. Then the rheumatologist ended with "find a hobby".

I had to get back to my songwriting because it made me happy and didn't require me to exert too much of my energy.

Atlanta was much different from Los Angeles, but I still needed to be around it. With being exhausted, I just didn't think I could do it and take care of Cyrus. I remember Tiffany J., with Meshach Management, saying through all her years in the music industry, "she wanted it". When her son was young, as a Mom, Ms. Tiffany J. expressed what she had to do, that she even brought her young son to the studio with her. She didn't allow or use being a Mom as an excuse to stop her flow. She instilled that fire in me, to really go after what I wanted.

I enrolled at SongU and other online classes with some of the best mentors in the game. I remember talking to George Matthews who allowed me to be honest and told some of his story. Even though Mr. Matthews was all the way in Cali, he helped me from afar and motivated me.

I had to do the very minimum which was to take care of myself and my son, but I needed money. Songwriting at the time was a hobby and can eventually bring money with the right team and hits. I was use to making my own money as an adult and not relying on my parents. I started networking again and tried to live normal. I've come to know normalcy doesn't reside with Lupus. I kept flaring up, mostly due to emotional stress and the emptiness with my husband back in Cali.

He decided to fly to Atlanta, even though it was difficult, I was determined to make it work. I wanted to be with my family and embark upon a fresh start. No money and sick, just added to the tension. Arguments didn't even need to happen, always found themselves center stage. I just wanted to alleviate both of our pain and anxiety, but I had to ask for help. Asking for help was the one thing I didn't want to do.

Since it became very difficult for me to work a full-time job, I needed to do something else than the traditional 9 to 5. I needed to work from home so I could rest on days I wasn't feeling well and still provide for us. Yes, my thinking was wrong at the time. I didn't need a traditional job but I surely needed a traditional husband to provide. I guess my actions confused him.

See the perception was I wanted to be the man, the head of our family and have all the control. My husband's thinking could not have been more wrong. I viewed my interaction as having things in their place. Being organized and sticking to an action plan just helps when dealing with any autoimmune disease, or just life.

My husband began cheating and I had a new job title, PI. I had to make some hard decisions, but he had made it for both of us. My husband chose to abandon me while I was on bed rest with pneumonia. I had no choice, but to let him go. I mean there I lay, could barely breathe, emotionally, nor physically.

My Mom found me in the room one day, opened the blinds and put the words on me.

""This isn't you! You're not acting like my daughter." My Mom blasted.

I cried and yelled, "I'm fat, broke, and my husband has left me! What do you want me to do?"

My Mom always gave tough love, no matter how broken I felt. "Well you're not going to just sit around and die. Get out the house, walk up the street and back, go do what you love and live." My Mom demanded.

After my high emotions calmed down I knew I had to get my mental right. I began to walk up to the front of the neighborhood and back for 15 minutes each day at the same time. I needed structure again. I started eating better and really taking care of myself. Oh, I was fine again! It was funny because I was being hit on.

My Mom would say, "Nobody knew you were skinny before. What they see is a woman."

Hey, I don't care, as a woman you need to be complimented and I was becoming my own woman again with my Mom's help. These were moments when I could say I should have listened to Momma, she knows everything. Sometimes I could get a whiff of her perfume, *Estée Lauder's "Knowing"* and know exactly what to do, almost like an approval. It was though I became fully aware of something.

You can sit and be pretty all day, but no one wants to be broke. My Mom, yet again had to divert my attention of all the endless possibilities. You're so good at administrative work and I may have a client for you. You can become her assistant and she knows about your diagnosis. This was the woman who got married the same day I was diagnosed, Mrs. Juanita Ann Bates, the owner of a Louisiana Hospital, with headquarters in

Atlanta. The one I call my natural healer and pain all at the same time.

My Mom must had talked me up so much and I only met her once before. I didn't even need an interview. The day I became her executive assistant, I worked in my own office in her Alpharetta mansion. The environment instilled beauty and drive in me to do well. I quickly became her personal assistant as well, travel, clothes and dining. She took care of me, healthcare was her thing.

Juanita became my personal health guru. She possessed humility about her I had never witnessed before. There were many incidences where I didn't feel well and didn't even need to go into the doctor or hospital because she knew exactly what to do. Whether with essential oils, a lymphatic massage or a steaming treatment with her very own drops she created and cared for me. Juanita really helped me understand I needed to take care of myself and in order to do I needed to educate myself more about the illnesses I was dealing with.

I was going back to school, while I was working for Juanita. This lady taught me many different aspects of the back office of running a hospital. One being medical coding and billing, you have to have great integrity for this position. I understood the data entry, but I needed to understand what and why I was doing it. So I enrolled at MedTech the following year so to become certified in that area. Also simultaneously learn more about the body, the anatomy and physiology to be more equipped to handling mine. Juanita taught me two more things which helped me over the years in life:

-To give myself a time limit for my emotions

-When you have an issue and it's known that is the fixed portion of the equation, so focus 99% on the variable, the solving; that's where you give your energy.

I had an amazing experience during my time at MedTech. It enabled me to understand more about the illness itself, the functions of the body, how they work, and how to take care of my own body's many malfunctions. I also was surrounded by many people who encouraged me to keep going, even when I had to sit out a month after another huge flare up where my heart began to shut down.

One of my instructors happened to be Vernice Haliburton, also a Lupus survivor. She was also an author I met the year before at a wine tasting fundraiser for Lupus. Ironically, the Winery owner who provided some of the wine also had Lupus. I became more accepting to my new lifestyle and having some courageous women around me made me feel victorious. There were times the school even made slight adjustments for me such as being able to wear my sunglasses or hat because the sun bothered me so much due to photosensitivity.

The impact of Lupus on the Body

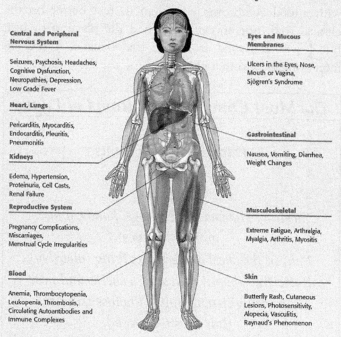

The Impact of Lupus on the Body

Central and Peripheral Nervous System

Seizures, Psychosis, Headaches, Cognitive Dysfunction, Neuropathies, Depression, Low Grade Fever

Heart, Lungs

Pericarditis, Myocarditis, Endocarditis, Pleuritis, Pneumonitis

Kidneys

Edema, Hypertension, Proteinuria, Cell Casts, Renal Failure

Reproductive System

Pregnancy Complications, Miscarriages, Menstrual Cycle Irregularities

Blood

Anemia, Thrombocytopenia, Leukopenia, Thrombosis, Circulating Autoantibodies and Immune Complexes

Eyes and Mucous Membranes

Ulcers in the Eyes, Nose, Mouth or Vagina, Sjögren's Syndrome

Gastrointestinal

Nausea, Vomiting, Diarrhea, Weight Changes

Musculoskeletal

Extreme Fatigue, Arthralgia, Myalgia, Arthritis, Myositis

Skin

Butterfly Rash, Cutaneous Lesions, Photosensitivity, Alopecia, Vasculitis, Raynaud's Phenomenon

Lupus can affect any part of the body; however, most people experience symptoms in only a few organs.

- Lupus is an incurable chronic autoimmune disease that causes inflammation in various parts of the body. The disease can range from mild to life-threatening.

- 90% of people with lupus are women, 80% of them developed lupus between ages 15 and 45.

- The cause of lupus is unknown. Scientists believe that individuals are genetically predisposed to lupus, and that environmental factors "trigger" the symptoms.

- With proper treatment, most people with lupus can live a normal life span.

My doctor was proud of me in how I went back to school and was working again. However, proud or not she was still concerned about my emotional stress and filing for divorce. I had to realize emotional pain was one of my top triggers for a Lupus flare. She recommended I try a clinical trial she was performing in her very own office. Even though I was managing my Lupus, I was still continuing to have too many flares with added symptoms. I began to feel better on the clinical trial, not knowing if I had the placebo or not, but I was removed from the trial because I had an infection prior to that eliminated me for the timing.

The Most Common Symptoms of Lupus

Headaches

Painful or swollen joints

Fever

Anemia

Swelling (Edema) in feet, legs, hands, and/or around the eyes

Pain in the chest on deep breathing (pleurisy)

Butterfly –shaped rash across cheeks and nose

Sun- or light-sensitivity (Photosensitivity)

Hair Loss (Alopecia)

Abnormal blood clotting

Fingers turning white and/or blue when cold (Raynaud's Phenomenon)

Mouth or nose ulcers

I continuously knew I had to keep finding ways out. When I looked up because I wasn't standing still or stuck anymore, I realized I had another Lupehole I had all along.

.

Lupehole #3: Support

The support I received from my family and friends was endless, even from some strangers. My support system began forming on its own. There's never a day someone is not supporting me in my journey or walk of life.

Self-Notes

How can you view and use your support system as a Lupehole?

_____

_____
_____
_____
_____
_____
_____
_____
_____
_____
_____
_____
_____
_____
_____
_____
_____
_____
_____
_____
_____

Walk

I had support from my family, but it was time I got support from those that understood my walk. The word walk, being an action and showing movement can usually refer to how you live your life, your path and or direction in life. I needed to know what I was up against to almost be prepared so while walking this purple bricked-road, I too would have my lion, tin man and scarecrow by my side.

I began to search for different Lupus support groups and thought it was a great idea and boy was I wrong! I signed up with so many all at once. It began to depress myself at seeing how much other people were suffering and my body couldn't handle the emotional stress. Thus, my symptoms only increased and I had to shut down. Then an epiphany, I met Carmen, the founder of Y.A.W.L. (Young Adults with Lupus). She really helped me see I needed to be around positive people and fighters. Carmen exposed highlights to everyone did not have the "woe is me" attitude. She encouraged me to come to the Lupus Walk held by The Lupus Foundation of America (GA Chapter) and to just see how much good support that exists. So my Mom and I signed up as walkers of the upcoming Lupus Walk in Atlanta with our own team,

"Float like a Butterfly," named after Mohammed Ali's famous poetic line while fighting in the boxing ring. It became even clearer to me; I too would be in for the fight of my life. We are all in a boxing ring and each of us has different opponents. I was determined to win, even if it was against myself. I needed to be a champion. I need to fight Lupus but gracefully just as the great boxer floated around the ring and stung his opponent like a bee. I too choose to float like a butterfly and spread beauty and a true essence of character like the legacy of the great humanitarian, Mohammed Ali left.

The day of my first Lupus walk, I met Maria Myler, the Chapter President and Teri Edmond the Program Director of the Lupus Foundation of America in Georgia. That day I decided to stay close to this organization for it was vital to have all the tools I needed. I was filled with so much gratitude all my family and friends were there. Just someone being "there" can make such a huge difference. From the signs to V-103, *The People's Station* blasting music, it felt like a celebration of life. When the actual walk begins, you are so overwhelmed with emotion like "we got this!" I felt elated to know people were rooting for me and it gave me courage more than anything! That first walk was a decision I will walk this walk and be a positive example for others. Remembering my Grams, Patricia "Ms. Patsy" Nassirou, her written song, "Make an Example out of me", I will do my best.

Then BAM! There comes a time even through your walk; you can become paralyzed by life.

At times I become emotionally paralyzed, enduring financial hardships, and even through unhealthy relationships.

I wanted to be a champion, but had to face the realization, I needed to have humility. I couldn't be in the ring alone. I needed to be equipped and trained through other's experiences to get me through and with this new found realization I found another Lupehole.

"The one walking with the wise will become wise, but the one who has dealings with the stupid will fare badly."

....Proverbs 13:20, walking shows intimacy.

...

At the 2014 Lupus Walk, GA Chapter - Atlanta

Lupehole #4: Other's Experiences

By sharing their stories, their daily activities and their do's and don'ts with me I began to get my very own set of matching gloves on. It wasn't just me anymore. I felt compelled to share their stories and just a few people that I have met that have inspired me to get through.

~Rochelle~

My name is Rochelle, and I have Lupus.
I was diagnosed with Lupus SLE in 2007. The indication was when I couldn't get up from the floor. Over the years, I suffered from joint pains, lupus flares, and rashes. My continuous prednisone usage for Lupus caused Avascular Necrosis. It damaged my hips and knees, so badly that I need bilateral replacement surgeries.

I was diagnosed with Lupus Nephritis in 2011. My kidneys failed in 2012. Thus I went on dialysis. However, I am blessed to have such a great support system. My loved ones give me the faith to move on. I believe that the Lord will have me healed in the future.

I'd say I have a few ways to escape reality. As a bona-fide nerd, I love to play games on my phone and new 3DS XL. My favorite genre is RPG or role playing games like Final Fantasy. I have a passion for reading and collecting mainly Marvel and DC comics. I live for comic book movies like Ironman. Lastly, I enjoy streaming anime on Hulu and Netflix. I've always loved the Japanese culture and I dream of visiting Japan one day!

Even though we get these illnesses, it doesn't mean we stop living. It's hard, but life is supposed to be that way. Listening to your doctor is great, but doing your own research too helps. I'd recommend getting a therapist to help your emotional health.

Honestly, I believe life is precious like Drake says YOLO, you only live once.

Lupehole

~Semi~

September 26, 2013 was when I was diagnosed with Lupus. It started with really bad chest pains. It felt like I had run a marathon and couldn't catch my breath. Doctors couldn't figure out what the problem was. Finally the doctors found fluid around my heart. When they decided to drain the fluid my lungs collapsed. I ended up on life support for 7 days breathing at 2% by myself. I was diagnosed with Rheumatoid Arthritis at the age of 13 and I couldn't understand why my fingers and toes were constantly numb and turning white and then dark purple... Which I eventually found out that it was another autoimmune disease called Raynaud's Syndrome.

I guess it all makes sense now...

On a daily basis, I have really bad joint pain, some days stairs are definitely a no. It's almost like my body has the flu. I'll shiver and sweat and feel really fatigue for no reason at all. Some days I'm okay. And I will feel healthy as can be on other days. The scary part is NEVER knowing, what my body will do next.

I've learned to manage my stress by reading more about healthy and herbal ways to manage my Lupus. I've accepted that I will no longer be able to do everything that I used to do and I try to figure out ways to do the things in a more Lupus-friendly way. It was hard letting go of the friends that I thought I had because they weren't willing to accept these changes, but at the end of the day a healthy me is a happy me.

When I woke up to a nurse pulling the life support tube out of my throat I KNEW my life had took a turn. The fall risk bracelet became my new jewelry, but it was the new me. The scars that were left on my body were the beginning of my new story. I couldn't believe I could no longer walk without the assistance from a walker , I couldn't believe I was connected to a 2ft oxygen machine, I didn't have enough strength to brush my teeth. I was at my weakest point in life but I was ready to fight for it back.

My advice to anyone living with an autoimmune disease is.... Understand that it's okay. It's okay to be angry, it's ok to cry and be frustrated that people don't understand what you are going through. But YOU must fight for your life! You must have the drive to continue ... Take your meds and read ...always ask questions and take notes at your doctor appointments. FIGHTING!

Lupehole

~Monica~

My name is Monica Ellis. I am the founder and CEO of Lupus Matters Corporation. I am a published author, a songwriter & producer. I have received many awards:

*2015 Jacquelyn Talley Lupus Fighter Award

*Awarded the Alliance for Lupus research bronze plaque for raising over $2,000

*LFA 500 club

*LFA 2000 club

I was diagnosed in April 2001 with Discoid Lupus and in November 2001 with Systemic Lupus. It took 7 months and one misdiagnosis before they said it was Lupus.

When I was first diagnosed I had never heard of Lupus, so I had to do a ton of research. I got connected with the Lupus Foundation of America. I started attending events and seminars. It helped me to understand what to expect but even knowing what to expect is nothing compared to actually living with Lupus. I was unable to work in my chosen field of Dentistry because it was too difficult to pass instruments to the dentist or sit for long periods of time.

I had a very active 5 year old that needed every bit of my attention but on many days I was way too tired and in pain to even get out of bed. I became less social and more depressed. Life as an active woman, working three jobs, hanging with friends and family became a struggle.

The way that I coped in the beginning was...I DIDN'T!!!! I was on 80 milligrams of steroids, Plaquenil, and Imuran and was prescribed Zoloft for depression.

So coping for me was a challenge, but with anything in life, you learn the do's and don'ts and what works for you and as time goes on you will flourish like the butterfly you are.

I have had Lupus for 15 years now, so there has been so many Lupeholes over the years. But there are a few that stood out over time:

80

Aleathea Dijon

1. *I know in my heart that God has saved me from Bad situations and death on a few occasions, but when he let me be diagnosed with Lupus, I really had to take a step back and ask myself, what am I going to do to inform people about Lupus? I feel like God allowed this, because he knows that I am strong enough to fight it and be a testimony for others too. I believe that we can still live life to the fullest.*

2. *My son is my heartbeat and he is the reason that I wanted to fight Lupus and live to see him accomplish things in life that a parent wants to see their child become. My son has been my rock through the whole 15 years of having Lupus. He has made me laugh when I wanted to cry, but he has given me strength when I wanted to give up. Even though he is 20 years old now, I still feel he is one of the reasons I am fighting so hard to LIVE with this disease.*

3. *Music is another Lupehole for me, it has gotten me through so much pain and devastation that Lupus causes. I'm not talking about the sappy love music, but referring to the ratchet, Hood, gangster rap music, it keeps my mind from wandering and becoming depressed, it helps me activate my day. LOL.*
When I think of music I think of these slogans:
Music makes the world go round.
Music only makes me stronger.
Music: My Anti-depressant.
Without music, life would not be fair.

4. *Another Lupehole that comes to mind is the people that I surround myself with. Having a strong support team is great. You need people in your corner that's going to love and support you because sometimes people with Lupus have a very hard time letting people know when we're not feeling so great. If you have people in your circle that knows your "Lupus language" and understand that there may be times that you don't want to be a bother or feel like a burden to others than you have a great support team.*

I'm going to be totally honest, right now at this moment in my life; my outlook on life can be somewhat of a roller coaster. I am

81

always going to be positive about living my life to the fullest and bringing awareness about this devastating disease, we call Lupus. So the one thing that I can say is always keep God first and prayer does work.

Just know what God has placed in your life and you can either crumble or you can CONQUER what he has put in front of you.

My advice to people facing any autoimmune diagnoses is to NOT panic because you will have the love and support you need from people facing your same struggles because YOU ARE NOT ALONE!!!

Trust me life will get hard and having an illness only further complicates things, BUT don't get discouraged because YOU are a WARRIOR that will CONQUER and DESTROY the likes of LUPUS!!!

Lupus Matters to us all...

Thank you for your love and support.

Aleathea Dijon

~Shasta~

I was diagnosed with SLE/Nephritis in April 2008 after a week, of undergoing numerous testing.

Challenges I go through on a daily basis are getting out of bed and not having any energy to do daily functions and tasks. I constantly have to choose doing one thing over the other and missing out on simple things such as hobbies and not being the normal social butterfly that I am.

I do a lot of resting and listening to music. My favorite is listening to water sounds capes to help me relax when I feel anxious or at night when I can't sleep.

My Lupehole is my children, they motivate me to stay strong and keep pressing forward for them and since my family members don't truly understand, all my "Lupies" in my support groups and friends are my Lupehole.

Also you have to have a passion. My passion and love for photography, fashion, and art are also ways that help me get through.

My outlook on life has changed tremendously. I value life a lot more because I almost died twice within a year after being diagnosed. My advice for anyone would be to put God first and don't feel bad when you can't always do what you used to do or have to rest when it's 20 things that need to get done. I had to learn how not to be Superwoman. Put your health first over everything and learn to listen to your body when you feel you're doing too much and know that 95% people will not understand and that's why we need more awareness. My hardships are not being able to work two and three jobs like I was use to and not being financially able to provide for my children, well teenagers like

I'd like to. Also, not knowing the unknown and what can happen next. It went from infected lymph nodes to pneumonia to spending three months in the ICU to catching a grandma seizure, and two hip replacement surgeries. The most recent Lupus flare caused kidney issues, bronchitis and pneumonia again all at one time, so God definitely has a purpose for my life and yours ....so never give up!

Aleathea Dijon

~Angelique~

I was a healthy 40 year old wife and mother of three awesome kids, living life day to day like everyone else. Going to work and just got the promotion of my dreams, taking care of my family, and enjoying life, so I thought.

Then it hit me like a Mack truck, BOOM! My life as I knew it changed. I was diagnosed with stage 5 kidney failure and a few days later Lupus nephritis of April 2013. After meeting my PCP for the first time late February 2013 she looked me directly in my face and said it looked like I had the onsets of Lupus. This was only after the first visit. I explained to her that I had an aunt who had Lupus as well. She set up some tests to be run and there I was giving vials and vials of blood.

I hadn't been feeling well for some time and just assumed I had the worst case of the flu ever. I was taking over the counter meds to treat myself like most of us do. One night, after being off work for more than two weeks, I thought I was going to go into work and told my oldest daughter, who is 18 at the time, to come with me. I was delusional because she did not have a driver's license, nor could she come to work with me. I wasn't in my right state of mind. We ended up at a hospital more than forty minutes away from our house, when there was one less than 15 minutes away.

During my wait in the ER I may have gotten up to go to the bathroom nearly ten times with no urine passing. The sensation of having to urinate and not being able to didn't register. After about a few hours it was my turn to be seen. After all the questions, drawing of blood, poking and prodding I was admitted as a patient. I was told that my kidneys had failed after they were unable to collect any urine by catheter. I was told the next morning that I had stage 5 kidney disease. I thought to myself: Are you talking to me? What did this mean? After two days in the hospital and now on dialysis I was told that I had Lupus Nephritis.

Lupus had aggressively attacked my kidneys. I was given steroids to try and stop the Lupus from attacking my kidneys any further. I had to go on dialysis because I wasn't passing urine on my own. When you are unable to pass urine on your own it builds up toxins in your body which is poisonous and can ultimately kill you. While in the hospital, I was scared and confused. I needed to talk to my aunt who had been battling Lupus for over 20 years. She gave me some advice and encouraged me to research the illness on my own. I was hospitalized for a little over a month. This disease became a life changing moment that I had not prepared for... I was out of work for nearly four months and had exhausted all of my sick and donated leave, as well as friends and family. Fortunately by the grace of God my kidneys reverted and I was able to stop dialysis.

Back to my story...

My job retired me disabled after nearly a year of being off. I miss my job and my co-workers. I worked hard to get in the position of Maintenance Mechanic. I enjoyed being one of the very few women to break into the "man's world" at the post office.

I have accepted what I have been dealt in life. My having Lupus is a blessing when I really sat and thought about it. God gave me the gift of gab to spread the word about this cruel disease. Since the passing of my aunt in April 2015 (died from complications of Lupus) I have been more inclined to spread awareness of this cruel disease.

I created KickRocksLupus on Instagram and Facebook to spread awareness and uplift those who don't see things in a positive light by having Lupus. My mission has been to make KickRocksLupus, a charitable foundation to help others less fortunate with everyday household needs, prescription costs, and to put those in touch with the resources needed. Spreading Lupus awareness like germs!

Aleathea Dijon

~Ron~

My name is Ronald K. Richardson Jr. I was diagnosed with SLE November 7, 1991. Also around the time Earvin "Magic" Johnson had made his announcement, which a lot of people confused the diseases because it affects the immune system. The challenges I have are nothing now compared to when I was first diagnosed. I was the star of a varsity basketball team and on a track team. I was very athletic, but I always had joint pain and kidney problem since birth. No one in my family had Lupus before or knew what it was. Even though I was a deacon at my church, my parents and own church family thought I was lying about my Lupus.

"Lupus had me on crutches at my senior prom," and many years I was called "Crater Face" not knowing I also have Discoid Lupus.

Even in college I use to pay someone to dress me to get to school, but I was determined.

Lupus caused a lot of problems between my parents, especially financially with medical bills. When I was young, I tried to help my parents and the way I got money is something I am not proud of, I just was hurt by seeing my parents cry in frustration and I felt like a burden.

I honestly believe and my friends tell me all the time, I could have definitely made it to the NBA. My outlet is going to the gym at 5 am and trying to shoot a little ball.

The advice I would give to others that are going through is not to give up, get through! Always have an optimistic attitude and know and understand it's not your fault.

87

Jersey #21

Since my diagnosis I have attended all the Lupus walks in Atlanta, GA. Sometimes I could walk and other times it was just nice being out at Piedmont Park with people that truly understood my day to day. It doesn't matter if you walk slow, or at your own pace, as long as you are moving. With one foot in front of the other

"I walk slowly, but never walk backward."
- Abraham Lincoln

I began meeting different ones and asked a lot of questions and not even realizing I had found one of the best Lupeholes anyone can ask for in life and that is getting something out of life by learning from someone else's experience and not experiencing it alone. No matter what you are dealing with, you will get through. I definitely now have the courage, the heart and the brains to walk this purple-bricked road. But be careful of the Lions, tigers, and bears, Oh my!

Self-Notes

How can you apply other's experiences as a Lupehole?

_____

_____

_____

_____

_____

_____

_____

_____

_____

_____

_____

_____

_____

_____

_____

_____

_____

_____

_____

_____

Pills, Pills, Pills

I became a lifetime movie. I was playing a role out loud, but in my reality, becoming something I'd tell myself I would never become. Lights, camera, action: I' remember watching it almost every Sunday growing up. There I was calling the women stupid. But that was me, I was her.

A tornado wrapped my psyche daily of the thoughts of unworthiness, so what would I do? Snap out of it or medicate? Medicating seemed to be my way out, but a false Lupehole. You really have to watch out for those false Lupeholes. I began to medicate because it was easy and it felt so much better, than any type of pain. Some days I could function and well others I was just there, a shell of a human body. I masked pain with false laughter and unwanted company. It became so bad I would go to multiple doctors to have enough supply. Yes, supply, because my demand was too high.

Dr. Richardson, I really need my pain meds! I'm in severe pain. The 800's are not working, I could take three or more and nothing happens. The pain is still there. I need morphine, Percocet, Vicodin.

I wanted the "good stuff," the high grade narcotics. I not only wanted to relieve my physical pain, but all the emotional pain I had along with life, the future, and the agony I didn't want to face. The thought of losing this daily battle with Lupus too soon haunted me. I yearned to go down the rabbit hole; it just "felt" better. Yet, that thought process was just another lie to myself.

I remembered I tracked down an old friend I knew who sold. I called him and asked to meet me. He refused and told me I had better figure it out another way. He made it clear there would be no meeting and he wasn't my pusher man.

So another no presented itself to me but I remember....not yet. I found my pusher man via the small clinics and I could get them fast. I had a legitimate reason and it was good enough.

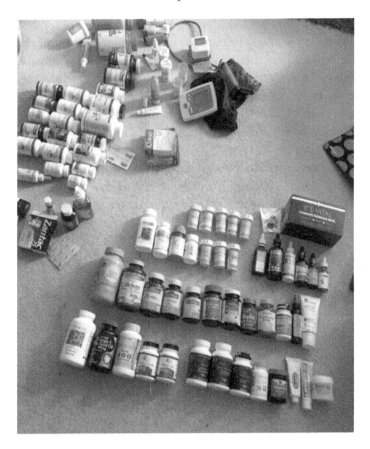

Taking a bath, I began to doze off and my cell phone was always near. It lit up and it was Meta. I sat up in the tub. I tried my best not to slur my words. I tried to act alert but I think I came off as a liar. She could tell I was keeping something from her, and I was. I just popped six pills and began to feel it, slouched down in the water.

"What are you doing? Why are you being weird?" Meta asked in an investigative mode.

"I will call you back," I said and rushed her off the phone.

I didn't call Meta back. I had no intentions. I remembered she had lost her aunt that way. I couldn't tell her what I was doing. I was more concern of how she would feel. I thought rushing off the phone with her would protect her feelings. Little did I know I was burying my own.

People do the strangest things in the bathroom. While others feel they are only in there doing what should be the obvious, but that's just not the case.

I really needed an escape and quickly. The pills were not working so I had a plan. I felt like no one knew my pain or understood it. When I would look in the mirror, it was not me I saw. The reflection in the mirror was someone who didn't need to exist. I felt I needed to eliminate myself. Even walking down a trail of destruction called suicide I try to hide the truth with a word like elimination. I found time to rationalize thinking I wouldn't be missed and my absence could solve a lot of problems and other's worries.

The hard truth of the matter is I was seeing a woman of my color, diseased, marital status; living conditions and financial bracket die every week. Death was all around me and embedded in my head. I figured I could just end this misery and hurt. After all, I would only be another statistic to pad the numbers of death. Really, who would care?

At this point I went to a doctor who really didn't know my medical history. I didn't care of his knowledge or sincerity regarding my condition; I was just seeking relief, well more pills. He recommended methotrexate, used as a chemotherapy drug and a DMARD for patients with Rheumatoid arthritis. I began taking the oral pills, come to find out later I was supposed to take it once a week with folic acid. This doctor had me taking it daily, with no real instructions. I literally wanted to die. I would wake and vomit, I would eat and vomit. I would be driving and vomit. Have you ever had to vomit and sometimes couldn't make pulling over? I have and it's not pretty. I would try to take a bath, but I would vomit, trying to stay in to be clean, but not able to stand. I would just let the shower water run while I sat there in whatever was inside of me, was in the tub with me. It was depressing. I was desperate so I took it, thinking it would make me better. I was neglecting myself as if I had deserved this ailment of mine. I questioned, "What did I sow?" Not only was it physical but a mental decline as well. Although my body or mind wasn't right, I knew how to smile through the pain. I learned this behavior from being in unhealthy relationships. Putting on face was easy. People would ask, but did they really want to know, help, or really care, I'd wonder? I became Smokey Robinson's song, Tears of a Clown, camouflaging my sadness became routine to normal.

I went back to the doctor again asking for better relief. He suggested I changed over from the pill form to the injections. So I followed orders with no questions asked. My Mom gave me the injections every Tuesday at 7pm. It was better, no more throwing up, but I walked around with nausea waiting for it to come up, something. I was on edge-every day.

I hit rock bottom when I began writing my suicide letter. I wished no one to leave like this and I didn't want to either. I told my family I loved them and please take care of my son. I stated and wanted them to just know I'm not in any type of pain now. I provided details of anything they needed to find out about me like passwords, bank accounts, where I left my ultimate black book. Oh how I cried and my body shook as I wrote every single word. I figured it was the least I could do as if I was doing everyone else a favor.

I had it all planned out. Everyone was already gone for the day out of the house. I just needed to get Cyrus to school. He would be there most of the day and someone else could pick him up, if they didn't hear from me. I had enough pills I could end my own life. It would be EASY, so easy.

Cyrus was ending his school year and we had always had a good routine. Every day it was said. I love you and have a good day to each other.

The day I was going to go through with my suicide plan, I didn't say a thing to my son. I just pulled up to the school, like get out. No words, no farewells, no "I'll see you laters". For some reason, Cyrus ran back to the car as if something was wrong, but he was fine. He flashed his BIG smile and his bright eyes!

He told me, "Mommy have a good day, love you," with both thumbs up. My darling son's eyes captured me and I held my tears back and said, "You too."

I knew at that moment I couldn't leave Cyrus. He had already had one parent abandon him, I couldn't do it. He didn't deserve that. GOD's Holy Spirit through my son saved me that day. My son ministered to me with such small words, with a simple gesture, but in an astronomical way. Cyrus was my knight. I went back home, retrieved the note and went to work.

From that day forward, people I come across I tell them, "Have a good day." You never know what kind words and gestures can do for a person. We don't know what others are facing, but you can minister to their spirit by almost commanding them; "HAVE A GOOD DAY!"

I say it now, everywhere I go: the grocery store, the elevator, and in passing. People are always questioning, "What is she so happy about?"

Remembering Whoopi Goldberg's famous line in The Color Purple, *"I'm poor, black, I might even be ugly, but dear GOD, I'm here. I'm here.*

During this time I began reflecting on life, not taking things for granted. From the smallest courteous acts like letting people over in traffic to just being there for my friends in the best way possible, I made a conscious effort.

Many know Bobbi Kristina passed away July 26, 2015 in a similar way her mother, Whitney Houston did because it was televised. In all those broadcasts what wasn't shown was the pain of the family members. That pain threshold is just something you can't broadcast. The day to day hospital visits and stays, not eating, and not showering. Even though I was going through my own ordeal I was still here, alive and had to be there for my friends. Whatever I could do to help, no matter how big or small, support was needed.

I knew the families through my relationship with Meta since I was 15 years old. Meta was like her second mother. She took care of her from while we were still in high school to even after having her own child, my Jayden.

Regardless if it was sleepovers, dinners, parties, or no matter what type of gather, they were so welcoming and made you feel like family. It didn't hit me until I went up to the hospital and saw the camera crews just waiting like vultures. This was not TV, this was very real and I couldn't do anything, but pray. You just feel helpless. I never once listened to the news, but only wanted to hear directly from the family.

How selfish am I? I am going back and forth about ending my own life, but here she was 22 years old and fighting for hers. Even though I'm only a friend of the family, like so many, it hit me really hard. Emotions were high and we, Meta and I even got into it the day of the funeral. We were both born in July. We are a lot alike, sensitive and love hard. I was angry there was nothing I could do. She was hurt because of such a great loss, another loss and knew what I was dealing with on chemo. When I got to the funeral I was calm and in good spirits, trying to be strong and we had made up with I love you and I'm here for you. We've been through too much and we needed each other. There were no ands, buts or maybes. That's my sister.

The service was beautiful, but once again bombarded with media. I sat next to some of Meta's other closest friends for support and like any funeral there were speakers who knew the family. I remember Mr. Tyler Perry looking out and saying, *"Don't take your DREAMS to the grave."* That hit me like a ton of bricks. I began thinking of my own future, my son, and wanting to live.

Something so simple that was stated with so much power. Those words from Mr. Tyler Perry remain in my conscience. Words can heal or destroy and impact your life in ways actions may not. I thought of how she wanted to sing like her parents and while we were in LA she would say, "You gotta write me something dope tho, "Baby Momma" as she called me, cuz I was always taking care of everybody's kids. Then another speaker got up, Dr. Toni Luck, a transformational specialist, author, and motivational speaker. I loved how she spoke, like directly to your soul, but with so much realness, and no hidden agenda. I remembered her, but never met her in person. Meta was like yea, I'm going to Israel. She had baptized the Brown family in the Jordan River years and years before.

At the repass, Meta introduced me to Dr. Luck and she learned of me having Lupus and on chemotherapy drugs. Dr. Luck talked to me for a bit then prayed with me. My entire body was hot like fire. , I didn't want anybody to become alarmed and questioned what did this women just do to me? I played it cool, because I would have been the one looking like a fool. So I casually just removed my white blazer and headed to the bar after thanking Dr. Luck for her kind words.

Death is a time to reflect on life, your life. Are you just surviving? What are you living for? The greatest achievements become our children, our legacy and what we leave behind.

From pills, pills, and more pills to chemotherapy drugs I had to look for a better future. What would be my legacy?

I didn't realize the entire time I had one of the best Lupeholes to add to the list; my son, my offspring, "Our offspring."

I wanted to die and he, my amazing son needed me to live.

Lupehole #5: Offspring

Our seed and our children are the byproducts of the very essence of who we are. Our GOD-given rights as parents are to think and act on their behalf and well-being. GOD gives us our children as a reflection of HIM and HIS Only-Begotten Son. We love GOD because HE loved us first [1 John 4:19]. In turn, our children love us because we love them. Through our children we learn so much. We discover how to really love. We learn love through patience, endurance, humility and so much more.

If you have a child, what have you learned? If you don't have any children yet, or choose not to, do you agree you can still learn from a child? Even at play, how unselfish they can be, or so innocent. They don't see color, race, or culture, but see a mere human being. They never question living, they just live. They don't

even look for validation perhaps because their existence is validation in itself.

Where down the line did you start seeking validation from others? Yes, we want others to be proud of us, but when we make Jehovah, our Heavenly Father's heart rejoice, human opinion seems so minute.

Children are precious and an amazing Lupehole.

Let us continue learning from them and allowing them to be an escape from daily life obstacles.

Self-Notes

God allowed us to procreate. If you have children or desire to have them one day, how can you use your offspring as a Lupehole?

_____

_____

_____

_____

_____

_____

_____

_____

_____

_____

_____

_____

_____

_____

_____

_____

_____

_____

_____

Lupus is difficult to diagnose because its symptoms come and go, mimic those of other diseases, and there is no single laboratory test that can definitively identify the illness.

Orange is NOT *the New Black*

I dropped Cyrus off at school and headed to work driving my regular commute up Highway 78. It had been raining so the roads were wet. I needed brakes and tires and payday was two days away. I thought to myself I could make it a few more days. I was driving as carefully as I could, not texting, and I even turned off the radio to pay complete attention to the road. When BAM! I hit the lil' red Corolla I had been trying to avoid. My head slams up against the steering wheel, and all I could think was "I hope the driver is okay." Confused, I didn't even realize it caused a four car pile-up. I jumped out of the car to rush and apologize asking the young woman that appeared to be in her early 20's. "Are you okay? Are you okay?" I asked twice.

She steps out of her car in house slippers, probably just to make a quick run somewhere and responds, "I'm okay."

The driver in the front of her she hit gets out and asks. "Is everyone okay? "I have no damages. I have to get to work."

The driver that rear ended me just leaves the scene. As I am talking to the young lady a police car was cruising by headed into work and pulls over to help.

The police officer questions us both and I take full responsibility, I take pictures of all damages and get back into my car. I was happy I just switched my car insurance to full coverage. Yes, I thought, I will just drag this car to work if I have to.

The officer says, "I am going to have to cite you for driving too closely."

This I knew since I couldn't brake quickly enough and I knew my tires were bad so I said, "Okay". After all, it was understandable due to my negligence and delay in keeping up with car maintenance and upkeep. So I get back in my car to text my coworker, Ky:

"I just got into an accident, I smashed the front of my car pretty bad, but I think it's drivable, I will be there ASAP."

The officer comes back to my car and says "Step out of the vehicle."

"Is everything okay? I have insurance." I respond.

"Are you aware you have a warrant for your arrest?" The officer informs.

"No." I said in disbelief.
"Place your hands behind your back." The officer ordered.

As cars drive pass, it seemed like a movie. The time seemed to have been turned on to like a switch to slow motion. I'm wearing all black, feeling like I was attending a funeral and I was the one about to be buried. Perhaps not like a movie but more of a bad nightmare. I was going to jail. I couldn't talk myself out of this one. How embarrassing.

Meanwhile another officer pulls up and says, "Let's just check everything out."

You know when two officers are there, you are definitely going in.

"It looks like you violated probation." The second officer said.

I said, "I was on probation, but I took care of that. I completed everything.

At this point I am pleading, "The information was untrue. I paid my probation. I did community service. What is this all about?"

"Sorry ma'am we have to take you in because it's not our jurisdiction." The officer informed.

I was in DeKalb County and the warrant came from Rockdale County. I thought it will be fine, as soon as I get to the jail I will call my sister and get bailed out. Easy, I did nothing wrong.

We pull up in the back of DeKalb County jail. A place I visited friends at and bonded out. Never did I

104

imagine I would be patted down like a real criminal and sitting in a holding cell on Memorial Drive. I'm so calm though because I'm handling this like business because that is when I am the most logical.

No emotion, just check off the task list and get it done. I sat there for hours, I became hungry. It had gotten cold. A lady officer finally comes and says you can make your phone call. I call my big sister, Shana and say, "I'm at DeKalb County and they have to transfer me to Rockdale County. When I call you from there just come get me out."

Without hesitation or worry, Shana says, "Okay and I'm good."

I'm thinking I took care of that. What's next? Hours and hours go by and now I have no sense of what time it is. A lady gestures to me, are you hungry? And with an exhausted attitude, I rolled my eyes. Not only does boredom strike, anxiety creeps in and my head began to pound. I try not to over think anything and I just start singing low to myself for comfort. Remembering music was my first Lupehole. I finally get picked up from a Rockdale County female officer.
I immediately ask, "What time is it?"
"13:15" the female officer answered.
"Were you in the military before this?" I asked.
"Yes."

While being cuffed again, I decided to hold a conversation and throw my attitude away to try to pass time. My Dad was in the military. He told me don't even think about enlisting. He knew all too well how they treated women in the military. Even 'til this day I can only imagine, but never wanted to find out.

"Do you like being an officer?"
"Yes, and no, I like to help people. But everything else I hate. So why are you in here anyway? You don't look like this is your thang."

"From what I know I had a warrant for violating probation after hitting another car. I'm going to call my sister when we get to next location and she will get me out. "I informed the female officer.

"Oh, no baby, I don't think it's that easy. I think if you violated probation, you don't just get out. You have to see the judge, but why were you were on probation in the first place?" the female officer questioned.

I just gave the easy but not the exposing truth, playing goody too shoes answer.

"Oh, same thing. I was following too close." I sheepishly divulged.

"With that you should be able to leave in a few hours. You drive crazy!"

I laughed. "I'm from Cali."

I felt relieved and we began discussing her future career plans as I sat in the back of her police car. I was always interested in how people chose their career, what their true passion was and where they were going.

We made a stop to pick up a "real criminal" at a nearby store, she was cursing and kicking.

"I can't believe this. I have to sit in here with you two black MF's."

She got in and I gave her a smirk.
"What are you smiling at?"
"If you don't know, I don't know." I responded.

Then I became silent to get though the rest of the ride.

We finally make it to Rockdale and they dealt with her first. The officer comes back for me.

"I have to put cuffs on your ankles as well before going in." the female officer informed me.
I could tell that it hurt her to do this. At this point I'm the "ok girl" to everything, I'm going to follow all the rules and play the nice card to get out of here quickly. It's two something and I need to make a call again to Shana. I need to ask her with all this paperwork before I get out and can she pick up Cyrus. More time passes and I am just looking at everything, everybody, every detail of the facility. A facility so it didn't feel like jail, but just something that had to get done. I decided to question the other women who came in; I always talk when I'm nervous. Well, I always talk. Just to get a sense of what the process was like.

I called my sister:

I have to stay to see the judge because I violated probation and there is no bond allowed. I'm not getting out today. I don't know when I'm getting out."

I finish up my phone call with ankles cuffed and waddle back to the dirty bench, with shortness of breath.

I sit back down and began to freak out, rocking back and forth to soothe myself. Now they know I am being booked I have to see the booking nurse.

A sweet, but tough Jamaican lady approached me.

"Were you injured?" the booking nurse asks.
"Earlier this morning I hit my head on the steering wheel from the car accident." I respond.
"And you haven't been examined?"
"No."
"Are you okay?"
"I'm just cold and my chest hurts."
"Why are your hands turning blue?"
"It's Raynaud's, you know like the syndrome."
"Your checks are red too."
"Yes I am having a flare up. It's called a malar rash, or butterfly rash that spreads from cheek to cheek across the bridge of my nose. I have Lupus..."
"Oh yes. Well you have to go the hospital. We can't keep you until we know that you are stable."

So the jail refused me with my condition. At this point I begin to hyperventilate thinking of all the horrible things that could happen to me while in jail. They removed the cuffs from my ankles and put me back in the police car.

The officer who picked me up was ending her shift but decided to stay with me. She said, "You seem kind."

The officer didn't realize I had Lupus; a family member had recently passed from Lupus and wanted to stay with me. She took me to the hospital through a special way for inmates. Oh, I felt so special.

As I got closer to the front, other emergency room victims stared at me. Once again I was humiliated, in pain like I was a criminal. I guess I was now since I was being escorted in handcuffs by a police officer. I would look at me the same way too. How judgmental we are as humans. My stress level was so high I began to flare, my Lupus symptoms began to increase in minutes. My heart was stressed and I began to hyperventilate again.

The female officer didn't leave my side, but it wasn't like a watchdog, she was genuinely concerned. She told them I had Lupus and they took me right away.

Again the nurses couldn't draw my blood, I was in fact dehydrated. My veins continued to collapse, four people tried the usually. I hadn't eaten or drank a thing all day.

Good thing my concierge nurse Nic Williams showed me how to find my own suggestions of a stick one time when we were all on a cabins trip. I calmed myself down so they could draw the blood needed to test for what I was afraid of. I had been here too many times. The anxiety rushed through my body.

The female officer said, "I see you're in pain. Is there anything I can do, like call any family? This doesn't look good.Whisper as many numbers to me as you can and I will leave out and call them."

"Just call my sister," as I struggled to whisper.
I was glad I knew it by heart. The female officer exited quickly, while the nurses tried to draw blood.

I felt my heart was about to explode and I might just die right there in Rockdale County hospital.

A nurse from New York appeared bold and in control. She kneeled in and looked at me.

"You need to calm down. Your heart is really stressed and I need you to breathe like you're giving birth. You have kids? The nurse asked.
A son." I answered.
"Well breathe like when you delivered him." The nurse commanded.

I began to think about Cyrus and knew I needed to get it together, more so mentally. I listened to that take charge nurse because she was known to be a magician with the needle. She got my blood and also instilled strength I needed to get through the nights.

"Understand you are going to jail, I need you to stay calm."

I overheard your officer on with her superior. He is on his way down. It's our job to get you back to booking, but I'm trying to get you better than stable.

110

A big beasty salt and pepper haired man approached me.

"I'm going to call another officer to relieve Officer Patrick, her shift is ending. How is your pain level?"

By then it was coming down to about a six.

The ER physician came and stated, "Her calcium levels are very low. We need to run more tests and keep her for observation. Due to low levels of magnesium too, her heart is stressed and we need to get her blood pressure down."

Once the team figured out what was going on, they pumped me with several IV's (Intravenous therapy) and got me stable.

Another officer came to pick me up and we headed back to the jail. I finally got booked and had to go through the whole process. I was weak. I told the nurse every single medication I currently had been taking.

"We won't be able to accommodate all of them." The nurse said.

Go figure. Jail is not really an accommodating place, but this is my health. They didn't seem to care. When I got arrested, they kept all my personal belongings. I told them to check my purse I have what I need. They had to check to see if they were in fact real prescriptions and then released them to the head nurse, which took a few days to confirm.

111

When the nurse tried to give me a TB, tuberculosis shot, I refused. I negotiated with her logically. If you give me the shot now, you're not going to know if I have it until 48-72 hours later with the skin test, so if I'm in population with the other women, I would have already spread this airborne disease.

I went in the back room with the female officer.

"Open your mouth." The female office commanded.

I had to change in front of her for the cough and squat test. I had on black lace and had to remove my undergarments.

"You're not wearing whites? Only if it's white can you keep it on." The female office informed.

I placed on the orange jumpsuit with nothing else on and remembered one of my favorite shows.

At that moment I realized this is not a fashion statement, this is not what I want to wear.
    Orange is supposed to represent happiness and cheerfulness. Orange is, to decrease depression, but putting that infamous orange jumpsuit on with those orange flip flops was beyond depressing. This is not "The Life." Orange is not the new black.

She handed me a toothbrush, a small tube of toothpaste, a brown cup, a red rubber spoon, (anything could be a weapon) and a very small bar of soap, with one raggedy rag. I was told to hold onto these items tightly. Even in jail people steal. Duh, bars only bring out who you really are.

Have you ever heard that it's the same boiling water that cooks an egg and a potato? One softens and the other hardens. When you're in a "hot" situation, it shows what you are really made of. I really didn't know what I was made of, but I was about to find out.

The mug shots were taken, and then I was fingerprinted for the second time. I really felt like an inmate. Then they placed me in a holding cell. They were keeping me in a holding cell due to my condition to keep an eye on me. I felt relieved I was not entering population. Being alone, I felt safe, but my mind told me differently. I sat there for hours trying to figure out who to call. I wondered who could find out when I would see the judge. I made over 100 calls and no one answered, but my sister. I didn't want to continue calling her, it wasn't fair and at $15 per call it wasn't cheap either.

A few days had gone by and there was not much I would eat. So I didn't. I tried to drink water, barely. So, I slept to past the time. I would sob quietly and then sleep. My mind went absolutely crazy, against what I had set to do and how I told myself how to think. Thoughts I never thought or imagined came into my mind; I was entrapped with my mind's mind.

Being isolated on any level will drive a person insane like a mad animal. I had a man to the left of me eating his own feces and another on my right constantly banging on the door screaming like in a horror film. It was like I was in an asylum, an insane one.

You really do become a product of your surroundings.

So I slept in. When I was up, I thought the worse. All I could hear was loud buzzers, slamming doors and officers chatting and laughing. Thinking they still get to live their life once they clock out.

Then I had to use the bathroom, correction restroom for there are no bathtubs in there. What would I do? Everyone could clearly see me including the men and I had nothing on under the pretty, bright, orange jumpsuit. I thought of my "fashionista", creative, interior design anything mother. I placed the sheet under my jumpsuit and tied it as a dress so when I went to squat all they saw was the sheet.As soon as I went to the restroom the men inmates pierced their eyes through the glass, as if they could see right through the sheet. I felt gross, like a show for them all to see and for FREE, ugghh. I figured I needed to get out of myself and like the slaves did, just do what I needed to do to survive. I had to survive my own thinking.

I cried silently for the first few nights. I would think, is my son okay? What about my job, will they let me go with no communication. How is everyone else? I began feeling sick all over again. The meds they gave me had worn off a day ago and I felt the burning in my joints, the numbness in my limbs, the aching in my mouth and chest.

Even though I was sleeping, my eyes were heavy. Like each blood cell was fighting its own war, and my body was the battlefield.

When you're out of options or no longer can rely on your own strength you have to find another Lupehole.

So I surrendered to who knew me best. I bowed to who could help me survive and get me out of this ordeal. For I wasn't sure how long I would be there or when the chance to make a plea to the judge would arrive. I began to tell GOD, "I'm done." This is the only type of giving up that is allowed; giving it up to GOD. At many times in our life's, we pray to GOD and ask HIM to help us with a particular situation, but we tend to take it back, thinking with our own strength we can handle it. We think maybe GOD is too busy or our matter is too small.

So this time . . . I surrendered.

Lupehole #6: Surrendering

I released it all to HIM at that moment and didn't take it back because THIS was way bigger than me. The raw truth was my little self couldn't handle it alone. I was no longer in control with anything. My strength and independence was not enough, it was nothing.

A few minutes later my door buzzed and two men were picking me up off the floor out of my boat, my temporary bed. Then a male nurse came in.

"We have to move you to population because a man came in with a more severe case. We need to watch him more carefully. So pack it up!" the male nurse ordered.

There wasn't much to pack. I trembled inside as he shackled my feet. I already thought about what I would do if someone tried me. I had worn my glasses that day. My plan was to break them and use them as a weapon. That's right, if I needed to, glass and all; even though I knew they were only polycarbonate material.

I also went in with acrylic nails, long red nails. Acrylic nails is just a polymer powder and monomer liquid combined, but if you bite your acrylic nail the right way it becomes very jagged with sharp pieces. I was determined to protect myself as best as I could. I was never a fighter, but in that place, you have to become something you're not. I had no choice but to be ready for the unexpected.

I quickly remember a story told to me. An exotic dancer was backed into a corner about to get beat up and robbed of her "earnings" because the accusers insisted she stole their money. Intelligent, clever, and witty all at the same time, she questioned them, what dividends did you have? They weren't sure how to answer, so they said, what do you mean, like $5's? Yea we had 5's, you stole. She replied I got 10's all night. Even though backed into a corner, she was more powerful and got out of it, leaving them dumbfounded. Remembering other's experience and through education could get you out, this time using multiple Lupeholes at once.

I entered the main campus for women and the guard asked, "What bunk you want?"

I strategically picked the one all the way in the corner just so I can see anyone coming my way. I sat down and just felt exhausted with the transfer. I spoke to no one, nervous and all, I thought it was best to just observe.

This time they gave me more to work with. When I was locked up I had cash on me, they allowed me to put that on my books for commissary. I told myself just because you are in here, doesn't mean be like them. I had to take care of myself.

Some women spoke, I just head nodded. I don't do that, where did that come from. They approached me, questioned me, "What's your name? Where you from? What you in for?"

I answered with short answers. I gave my government last name, Cali and said I was following too closely.

"Like in a car."

"Yea."

"That's stupid!"

One girl pretty much was a jail bird and said, "Nah she's in here for more than that."

"Well I violated my probation, not sure how."

"Oh you have to sit here for a long time."

My Bunkie interrupted, "No you won't. Do you have any underwear?"

I guess she was being "nice". It is not a very trusting situation, but I had none and she handed them to me. Take them, they were just washed. When she smiled her teeth were like brown and black clay. She was a meth head and had to be transferred to prison soon, so she began her journey of change already to help others and "be good" for selling too much of it. She could never explain the amount or the how long.

I just sat there, like I am really in jail. I kept telling myself don't change who you are. I kind of just figured things out. I headed to the kiosk. Yes, a kiosk I guess for communication purposes to check on my case, ask questions to the customer service and order some items off the commissary:

Oatmeal
Toothpaste
Dove soap bar
Cocoa Butter Lotion
Granola bars and paper

I needed paper, I needed to write.

I wasn't sure how long I was going to be in, so I was stingy and ordered just a few things.

When I started thinking how my day would go, that got interrupted by a guard telling me how my day would go, when to eat, when to clean, when to sleep.

I had someone else controlling my schedule, my day, my life. I started to feel helpless again and thought of really how did any type of slave feel? There was no escape this time behind these walls. My schedule was:

Up by 4am for check and eat breakfast
Then lunch was served at 10am
Then dinner at 6pm
Cleaning duties completed after dinner
Medicine call at 10pm
And lights out at 11pm after another check
Good Night.

118

I couldn't adapt, but as long as I followed the rules, let's say, I modified my day.

While the others got up and ate breakfast, I stood for check and then got back on my metal flat framed with a crate pad to sleep.

A guard came to me and asked, "Why are you not eating,"
I responded, "I have health issues. I can't eat that. Quickly other inmates recognized and asked for my plate. I agreed if I got something in return. The guard requested I see the nurse again.

I saw the camp nurse and explained to her I had Lupus and a few other autoimmune diseases and she says, "Oh like you can't eat gluten. I will order a "special tray."

I didn't correct her and I didn't decline.

Even though foods with gluten do cause a lot of conditions, I didn't' have many problems with gluten. I only knew about celiac. One of my friend's mothers had it, so I knew how this would go. I was actually excited to see what I would get at lunch. Man, the small things in life that make you smile.

Hours past and it was lunchtime but for me it was breakfast, 10:00 am like clockwork. They called me by my last name and you know me I turtle-styled across the floor. The guard yells, "Hurry up!" and inmate shouts, "She's sick!" in a way defending me.

Everyone's eyes were frozen on my tray. I got to pick and choose what I was going to eat from the tray, and the other women whispered what they wanted off of it. I ate healthy. I ate the fruit and the vegetables. No meat, no bread and anything else I didn't see before, I guess they called it MUSH.I gave that away and they loved it. The more meals I had, the more things I accumulated. I now had two pair of underwear, long john bottoms and a top. I got a fresh pair of socks and dishes to make food in. You have to play it smart.Bartering is sometimes the way to go. It's business. You do something for me and I will do something for you, and if all goes well, respect comes along with it. All I had to give was my tray, but then I thought I have something else to give.

Things got crazy, once I started speaking to the women. Like I said I wasn't going to change who I was. Even in there I carried myself with respect and let them know what I was going to do if I was tried, little ole me, but only if they tried me. It's just like poker though, I'm glad I was taught that game. You only tell the other players what you want them to know and on the other hand you may just be bluffing.

I started talking to some of the women and they had ideas, dreams and families. Some of them just wanted someone to listen to them. So I played games, read books, checked the kiosk a million times and listened to them.One lady came to me crying.

"They took my kids. They took my kids!" She repeated.
"Calm down and sit on my bed." I said compassionately.

A sign in there was if you let someone sit on your bed you welcomed them, somewhat like welcoming someone into your home.

"My kids were taken from my husband because he was on meth." She explained.

"Did he also do it?" I asked.

She answered, "Never. They had no right to take the kids from him and he failed a urine test."

"You need to call your attorney and ask them to do a blood test and or a hair follicle test. When one person does meth and is around another, the residue seeps into other's pores, even remains on the walls." I advised.

"How did I know that and why should she believe me." She asked.

"I took a drug and alcohol class as an elective in school for an abuse counselor years before." I answered.

She called her attorney and I hoped the best for her family. Well, that they could get the kids back to family members at least. It's hard to trust an addict, but something in her eyes and the cry for her children compelled me to speak with her. I felt like it's not in my hands, but I was glad to help ease her pain even for just a little while.

I witnessed this in my own family. Children ripped apart from my arms from bad decision making and addictions that controlled them. I never wanted to be in that situation and I promised myself that for my son to be the best mother I could be.

By this time I had to be clever about showering, for that was my peace for ten minutes. I showered from head to toe with that Dove bar with my orange slippers on and sang the whole time. I noticed everyone would go back to sleep after ten o'clock lunch and I was still up, so score! I had the shower to myself. I made it work, 'til one day a butch girl, tried it.

I turned and she was just there. I simply said, "Can I help you?"

To my surprise she did needed help, she said, "Can I step into your office when you get done?" the butch girl asked.

Nervous as all get right, I said, "I have an opening around TV time."

The Butch girl walked away staring of course.

It was a good meeting. I got all her information, and even though she was going away to prison for some years, I was able to help her. She seemed disturbed and confused about many things. After speaking with her I spoke to an older lady who was an author of a book about mental illness and how her husband killed himself.She was in for allegedly setting up home health care facilities for mentally ill patients and not handling the funds from the disability correctly. She explained to me that the "Butch girl" I was talking to had many mental illness issues, to be careful. I took her advice and learned more about mental illness, which had ran in my family. Another topic many don't like to discuss or to seek help for.

I never saw a problem with seeking help from a professional. To me it's just like you go to a hairstylist or a personal trainer. They are trained, skilled, and educated in places you may not be. I couldn't wait to make an appointment with my Counselor. Not only did she let me vent, but she gave me the tools to cope and to separate tasks and emotions to help when becoming overwhelmed.

One of those tools was a four quadrant Urgent/Important chart.

Anytime that you become overwhelmed with finances, this can help with paying bills. When you are dealing with an emotional feeling and or decision, this will help prioritize. When trying to manage your time and even your physical health, this simple chart can put so much into perspective. Get it out, off your mind and on paper, so that you can see it and compartmentalize. Not that you have to pull it out every time a situation arises, but become familiar with what is most urgent and important. I knew in that space there was not much for me to do, but to keep check of my mental state and plan what my next moves were when I got out.

That night we prayed, so we could sleep with some type of peace. We all had a lot on our minds and didn't know what the next day would bring since some had court the next day.

Stephen Covey's Urgent vs. Important Four Quadrant for time management matrix

	URGENT	NOT URGENT
Important	Quadrant 1 Crises Pressing Problems Deadline-driven projects	Quadrant 2 Prevention, capability improvement Relationship building Recognizing new opportunities Planning, recreation
Not Important	Quadrant 3 Interruptions, some callers Some mail, Some reports Some meetings Proximate, pressing matters Popular activities	Quadrant 4 Trivia, busy work Some mail Some phone calls Time wasters Pleasant activities

All I knew, was even in that situation, I had to remain positive.

I constantly replay the question of how I got myself into that situation in the first place and how it takes only one decision to affect your entire life, with a domino effect.

I realized I was going to keep this feeling of doubt in myself and fear of the unknown because of all that I had done and I would eventually have to reap even more of what I had sown. I knew this rain cloud would stay with me, wherever I walked. I just wanted peace. I knew exactly where to start to get a sense of peace.

This is what Jehovah says, your Repurchaser, the Holy One of Israel: "I, Jehovah, am your God, The One teaching you to benefit yourself, The One guiding you in the way you should walk. If only you would pay attention to my commandments! Then your peace would become just like a river And your righteousness like the waves of the sea.

I knew I had to not only surrender, but pay attention to GOD's commandments just like Isaiah 48:17-18 says. I wanted my peace like a river, long-lasting, and I wanted my righteousness to be like the waves of the sea, continuous, but I needed to and ask for forgiveness first.

Self-Notes

How can surrendering be a Lupehole?

_____

_____

_____

_____

_____

_____

_____

_____

_____

_____

_____

_____

_____

_____

_____

_____

_____

_____

Fear of Forgiveness

It came a point in my life that all I did was thank GOD for food before I ate, just out of habit and not really talking to him anymore. Like friends that only kept in contact for that "one thing." I was just here and dealing with whatever came my way on my own. I had put GOD on the backburner as if I could handle everything and didn't need him.

My life seemed to have had a trickle-down domino effect. One thing after another and I couldn't keep anything together. The stress was taking a toll on my heart and lungs and I had no peace. I could barely function, barely breath. I was allowing Lupus to take over. The feelings of suicide came back up, but I had to remember Cyrus. I had to keep fighting that feeling, but truthfully, it may sound weird, but even my son wasn't enough. If you have ever just felt numb to life, that was me. I became unresponsive and had no sensation, or willingness to do anything.

I didn't care anymore about my actions or who I hurt, as long as I felt good. I needed to feel good. The pills would always wear off and I would still be filled with empty. I knew what I needed and yearned for, but I was just too afraid to ask. I needed forgiveness from my Heavenly Father. Just like a child, I felt like I couldn't go to Him to ask for anything because I was too ashamed. I was in fear of being rejected and once again felt unworthy.

Did Jehovah forget about me? I would constantly ask myself. I thought if He did, I made it easy for Him to do so. I was sinning from the opening of my eyes in the morning to my insomniac thoughts at 3 am. I was so afraid of making another mistake or failing I would just not ask. I continued to drift away. I just would get further away from asking Him until a dear friend said this:

"When you DON'T ask GOD for forgiveness, you are saying to Him, thanks, but no thanks for sacrificing Your Son." You can acknowledge the sacrifice, but without action, it's like you are accepting a gift and never opening it, which shows it means nothing to you.

It was harsh, but true. I could no longer dismiss the sole purpose of Jehovah's sacrifice of giving up His Son, Jesus for us as a ransom, the life we could have had now, if Adam would have obeyed. That He loved us so much that if we exercised (thus showing action) faith in Him we would have everlasting life, the real life. I had death on my mind so much, I had forgotten about the gift of the real life. I forgot to rely on Him. That was my only failure. Failing to remember Him and know the type of GOD, Jehovah truly is.

I didn't want to be alienated from GOD anymore. I had some work to do. I mean some challenging, painful work. I had one of the best conversations with my Dad on the other end. He always gives the best advice without scolding while I lay on the bathroom floor. My Dad said one thing to me that put me in motion.

He said, "Dawta, there is no gray area in serving Jehovah, you need to make a decision."

So I made a decision to ask not knowing that this Lupehole you have to use daily, incessantly. The only way I could ask for forgiveness was by approaching Jehovah in prayer.

Lupehole #6: Prayer

I had to ask for forgiveness from the Almighty. At Psalms 86:5 it says *GOD is ready to forgive*, how encouraging. GOD doesn't chase us, but he waits for us. I was almost ready.

I also had to ask for forgiveness to those that I hurt and also to forgive those that hurt me. Ephesians 4:32 says *but become kind to one another, tenderly compassionate; freely forgiving one another just as GOD also by Christ freely forgave you.*

If you want forgiveness, you have to forgive. Simple I thought. Then I thought I was ready, but there was still this feeling of uncertainty.

"You will know that forgiveness has begun when you recall those who hurt you and feel the power to wish them well."
-Lewis B. Smedes

Forgiving ourselves is the most difficult, but I was determined to be repaired and be healthy in all aspects of my life. Our emotions can cause us many physical ailments. In one emotional chart it showed if you were holding on to grudges you could be the cause of your own joint pain and stiffness, which is a major symptom of both, Lupus and Rheumatoid Arthritis. Yikes! The body does not lie. Psychological stress can definitely takes its toll on all systems of the body.

Many different factors influence the experience of pain, which is different for everyone. These may include:

- *Age*
- *Gender*
- *Culture*
- *Ethnicity*
- *Spiritual beliefs*
- *Socio-economic status*
- *Emotional response*
- *Support systems*
- *Life before pain onset*

Other factors can include a learned response, which can be related to the response of your family. Parents, for example, may respond to a child's pain in a certain manner, setting a foundational pain response for an individual that may influence future pain experiences. Also, societal and medical care systems can impact the pain experience.

Have you ever notice how well some function under a lot of stress and then others do not? How some can get over a break up and other's wallow. The Emotions and the Chronic Pain Cycle is just that, a cycle of continuous processes repeated. Unless you figure out how to bridge the gap in a linear way in order to create your Lupehole out.

Aleathea Dijon

Emotions and the Chronic Pain Cycle

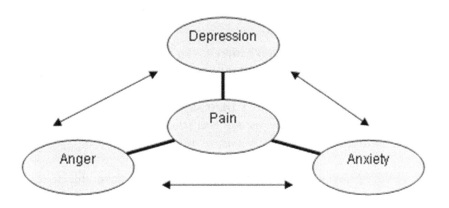

I knew there was some things I COULD NOT change about me such as: what happened before this emotional and chronic pain, my age, gender, ethnicity, which plays a huge role in my diagnosis, but I knew there was something I could do to minimize the pain that came along with it. That was checking my emotions. Checking our emotions, doesn't mean acknowledging them, but working on them and putting them in their proper place. Ecclesiastes 3:4 says that there is "a time to weep and a time to laugh..." We have many emotions, but controlling them and not allowing them to control you is essential.

Especially being a woman, an emotional creature, I had to begin learning the process of controlling my emotions and being on medications that alter my moods. I had to take some additional steps and reach out for some therapy, to even help with being a better communicator, because I couldn't do this alone. I

131

didn't want to go to family or friends, but a professional in the sense that they would work for me and with me, at my own pace.

I needed to forgive myself. To accomplish this need I was shown two important scriptures to me at the most perfect timing of my life, even though they had always been there. At Isaiah 1:18, it says *"Come, now, and let us set matters straight between us, "says Jehovah. "Though your sins are like scarlet, they will be made as white as snow....*

I really had to think about that and take this to heart, here Jehovah is asking us to set matters straight, even though I did the wrong and I vividly could see something so red, turn to white, as if it didn't happen, a complete reverting, wow!

And Acts 3:19 goes onto say *"Repent, therefore, and turn around so as to get your sins blotted out, so that seasons of refreshing may come from Jehovah himself....."*

He knows we are made from dust and we may fail, but I was signing up for some refreshment. Just reading it put my mind at ease. If GOD really watched every single transgression we made, we would drop like flies, but our sins would be blotted out? That's true forgiveness!

If you want a Lupehole in life, especially with yourself, you must be quick to ask for forgiveness through prayer. I was seeing that if Jehovah can forgive me, I can forgive myself, but I needed to do a little more work. There will always be a two-fold method to this Lupehole. In order to be free and out of that contract of resentment, holding on to just "stuff" and

truly be forgiven you have to work in harmony with
what you pray for. It's not always easy, but you have to
have **Obedience.**

Pray & Apply! Obedience will help you get
through with amazing results. Happiness! *Happy are
those conscious of their spiritual needs,* Matthew 5:3 proclaims.
The opposite of feeling unworthy, being proud of
yourself and knowing that you are so WORTH it,
especially to GOD! Satan loves to play on our emotions
to keep us sick, spiritually, emotionally and physically.
However, GOD is ALL powerful. Don't forget who
the real enemy is. We recognize his tactics and schemes.
There is no BRAVE, if you're not afraid as my son says.
However, having the correct type of fear, a healthy fear;
reverential awe of the Creator we can get through.
Wait, I think I found another Lupehole. Remember we
serve a happy GOD and life is like a song.

Self-Notes

How can you use prayer along with obedience as a Lupehole?

Early detection and treatment is the ley to a better health outcome and can usually lessen the progression and severity of the disease.

At Last

Sometimes I feel I am still on that bathroom floor. Now when I get up, I'm not getting up alone. I get up with GOD's help – **John 14:16**. I must remember the future days will have their own anxieties.

At Matthew 6:33-34 it says, *"Keep on, then, seeking first the kingdom and his righteousness, and all these [other] things will be added to YOU. So, never be anxious about the next day, for the next day will have its own anxieties.*

We don't know what the next day will bring, but we can be assured we can and will get through. Looking back at your years, you can ask yourself not just "Why Me?," but you can smile back and say thank You GOD "At Last" for getting me through daily and being my true escape and refuge with our intimate relationship, you have never left me. In order for me to be strong I needed to fortify myself and stay anchored so I wouldn't drift away again. I needed GOD's love to get me through then and the years to come.

I continuously remember my July vacation to Eastside Medical and how Jehovah was there for me. Going into stroke zone with blood clots, and breathing at 5%, Barbara all the way in California sent me Isaiah 41:10 & 13, which says:

"Do not be afraid, for I am with you. Do not be anxious, for I am your GOD. I will fortify you, yes, I will help you, I will really hold on to you with my right hand of righteousness.' .... For I, Jehovah your GOD, am grasping your right hand, The One saying to you, 'Do not be afraid. I will help you.'

I thank Him for using her that day as puddles gathered on the hospital floor. I didn't know I could cry so much.

So I had to review that contract I had signed on November 11, 2011 (11/11/11), but this time I had one of the biggest attorneys of them all walking with me into the courtroom for a new judgment holding my right hand, which was my ultimate Lupehole in life.

Every great attorney knows there's always a way out of a contract. I began to allow GOD to be my Great Attorney. I had to remember whatever I put first, was my god and just like an attorney to win your case, you have to be open and honest, and so they can use every angle necessary to get you out. Allow GOD to be that Lupehole for you.

The ultimate, continuous Lupehole is GOD.

So, let's look at the contract, the circumstances, and the reality of it all.

Aleathea Dijon

Life-Threatening Contract

This agreement made this 11th day of November by the named Healthcare Provider, and Aleathea Dijon.

Purpose of Contract. – To diagnose 2nd party with a life-threatening disease, namely Lupus, along with other autoimmune diseases over a period of time to debilitate her health and keep her enjoyment of life to a minimum.

Term of Contract. – The term of this Agreement shall commence on 11/11/11. After she gains a full understanding of the opposition, only then will this contract be expired.

Payment. – 2nd party will pay for all doctor's visits, with or without medical insurance, also; all medications and clinical trials so that we may continue to research. We also need the 2nd party to collect funds on account of our lengthy research. To pay with rears, and excruciating daily.

Risk Share Arrangement. – We have no risks on our end because we are backed by the top pharmaceutical companies and our degrees by accredited universities. 2nd party is at high risk including death, but is able to use any backing seems fit to reduce risk factors, if available, but are not in our findings.

<u>Responsibilities of Contractor.</u> – To diagnose, run tests, keep 2nd party ill in order to provide more medications to make astronomical profits.

<u>Signed by:</u>   <u>Signed by:</u>

_____   _____
Aleathea Díjon   Healthcare Provider

Life -Threatening Contract

This agreement made this 11th day of November by the named Healthcare Provider, and Aleathea Dijon.

Purpose of Contract. – To diagnose 2nd party with a life-threatening disease, namely Lupus, along with other autoimmune diseases over a period of time to debilitate her health and keep her enjoyment of life to a minimum.

Term of Contract. – The term of this Agreement shall commence on 11/11/11. After she gains a full understanding of the opposition, only then will this contract be expired.

Payment. – 2nd party will pay for all doctor's visits, with or without medical insurance, also; all medications and clinical trials so that we may continue to research. We also need the 2nd party to collect funds on account of our lengthy research. To pay with rears, and excruciating daily.

Risk Share Arrangement. – We have no risks on our end because we are backed by the top pharmaceutical companies and our degrees by accredited universities. 2nd party is at high risk including death, but is able to use any backing seems fit to reduce risk factors, if available, but are not in our findings and research.

Lupehole

Responsibilities of Contractor. – To diagnose, run tests, keep 2nd party ill in order to provide more medications to make astronomical profits.

Signed by: Signed by:

Aleathea Dijon

_____   _____
Aleathea Dijon   Healthcare Provider

There were several Lupeholes in the contract provided:

The contract states for "a period of time," meaning that this agreement would have an end timing.

Then the contract mentions after gaining full understanding of the opposition, the contract will also expire.

This agreement also stated that there was the ability to use "any" backing to reduce risk factors because in their research and billions spent, they have found none.

And as you look closely, the contractor, the Healthcare Provider never even signed the contract, because they do not have the last say so, but only mere suggestions.

You see, not reviewing my contract, or knowing the terms, I signed it. I just accepted the agreement, because I thought I had to. Now I see why my mother has told me be careful and tread this earth lightly. If you agree to something and you think it's too late. I am here to tell you that it's not. There is always a Lupehole.

Jehovah has served as the ultimate Lupehole for me because with Lupus and living life, I know there will be more trials to come, more downs, losses, and hardships. However, the amazing love he gives me, the support and the drive to help others is amazing. I can teach others through my own experience, but the real deal, the real get through. I am able to assist and advocate for others in their trials of living with Lupus. I guess you can say I'm a paralegal and helping put "peace" back together.

I have shared my Seven Lupeholes, and I am sure by now you have found your own, really analyzing your own contract, whether you signed it, ripped it, or burned it up. You can start anew.

When I look back at the Seven Lupeholes I continue to use:

- *Music*
- *Self-Worth*
- *Support*
- *Other's Experiences*
- *Offspring*
- *Surrendering*
- *Prayer (w/ obedience)*

I realized how amazing that none of the Lupeholes cost, most are not tangible, but eternal. Lupeholes we all have access to. **Let's keep finding more to LIVE life!**

Self-Notes

How can GOD serve as your ultimate Lupehole to Life? Write why you're thankful and answer your question of "*Why Me?*"

_____

_____

_____

_____

_____

_____

_____

_____

_____

_____

_____

_____

_____

_____

_____

_____

_____

_____

_____

_____

_____

Autopilot

Now that I had found some Lupeholes in every area of my life and became more aware of how to overcome daily obstacles including my own body's malfunctions, I had to keep up with and apply what I had learned. I needed to transition into autopilot. I wanted to enjoy living!

Some tasks are routine to us like brushing our teeth, and some things are involuntary and we just do them. Living with Lupus, however, takes a greater effort in taking care of yourself. Knowing your triggers and paying close attention to your body and mood also play a major role in living your best life with any autoimmune disease.

The Most Common Lupus Flare Triggers

Extreme fatigue (exhaustion)
Weather
Stress
Poor Nutrition
ultraviolet rays from the sun
ultraviolet rays from fluorescent light bulbs
an infection
a cold or a viral illness
exhaustion
an injury
emotional stress, such as a divorce, illness, death in the family, or other life complications.
anything that causes stress to the body, such as surgery, physical harm, pregnancy, or giving birth

While a person's genes may increase the chance that he or she will develop Lupus, it takes some kind of environmental trigger to set off the illness or to bring on a flare.

Other Lupus Flare Triggers

sulfa drugs, which make a person more sensitive to the sun, such as: Bactrim® and Septra® (trimethoprim-sulfamethoxazole); sulfisoxazole (Gantrisin®); tolbutamide (Orinase®); sulfasalazine (Azulfidine®); diuretics

sun-sensitizing tetracycline drugs such as minocycline (Minocin®)

penicillin or other antibiotic drugs such as: amoxicillin (Amoxil®); ampicillin (Ampicillin Sodium ADD-Vantage®); cloxacillin (Cloxapen®)

Always get to the source of an issue and focus on taking care of yourself. When your body is telling you something is not right, be sure to listen.

I looked at taking care of me as no longer as a selfish act, but loving myself enough so I can be here to love and help others.

I also had noticed certain foods caused an increase in disease activity, such as acidic foods causing oral ulcers or my GERD would become agitated. So I had to keep a personal journal, noting what outside factors would cause my flares and what I could do to decrease them. I compiled a list of things that have helped and hopefully they will help you too.

Consult your physician or specialist before using any of the suggestions, these are simply products and foods I presently use or avoid.

Feel Free to visit websites provided to get more information about products.

From Scalp to Sole
*an item usually kept in purse for daily use

Hair
Alopecia
Dry scalp

A good hairstylist on stand-by (meaning they know about alopecia, a nice gentle, but stimulating shampoo/conditioner)

Moroccan oil – dry-no-more professional scalp treatment www.moroccanoiloil.com

The Skin (largest organ of the body)

Facial – olive oil serum used as an anti-oxidant Sonoma Naturals www.dermpeuticsinc.com

External Anti-inflammatory
Organic Pure Borage Seed Oil, Cold Pressed

Skin protectant – CVS brand zinc oxide 20% protects chafed skin – Usually use for my ears. www.cvs.com

Cortizone•10 Ointment or CREME with ALOE 1% hydrocortisone used for anti-itch, inflammation and rashes www.Cortizone10.com

*Sunscreen for Daily UVA/UVB Protection
Obagi Nu-Derm® Sunscreen Lotion; Broad Spectrum SPF 35

Healthy Skin Protection – 7.5% octinoxate and 9% zinc oxide.
Recommended by the Skin Cancer Foundation
www.obagi.com

Sunscreen for Travel/Vacation UVA/UVB Protection
Caren Original – Citrus Sun SPF 50 – 3% Avobenzone, 13% Homostate, 5% Octisalate, 2% Octocrylene, 4% Oxybenzone
www.carenproducts.com

Daily Dry Skin Therapy
Eucerin Moisturizing Crème Fragrance Free
www.EucerinUS.com

Also cover soles freely and place cushion socks on to absorb and lock in proper moisture, but not too much.

Essential Lotion
Two Old Goats – Arthritis & Fibromyalgia, used as a skin moisturizer and joint relief from pain and stiffness.
0.05% Lavender & 0.01% Chamomile (Relaxant)
0.02% Rosemary, 0.02% Eucalyptus, 0.02% Peppermint (Anti-inflammatory) & 0.01 % Birch Bark (Analgesic
www.twooldgoats.com

*Hand Sanitizer
EO® 62% Organic Ethanol Antiseptic
www.eoproducts.com

Feet & Heels
Vitamin Zinc repairs cracking
PRoFoot Heel Rescue Foot Cream with Moroccan Argan Oil
www.profootcare.com

Rx only
*Voltaren Gel – 1% diclofenac sodium topical gel

0.05% Alclometasone Dipropionate Cream

Eye Care
*Crying and Artificial Tears for Lubrication

Staying away from Ultraviolet lighting and the sun as much as possible

*ALWAYS have a pair of Hollywood (Big) Shades due to photosensitivity.

Nose
Sores – Vaseline and Q-Tip, I normally just let them go away on their own

Oral
*Fever Blisters/ Cold Sore – Abreva (Docosanol) Cream Pump
www.abreva.com

*Daily use of lip balm - Carmex 1.7% Camphor, 0.7% Menthol

Mouth Ulcers - Instant Mouth Sore Relief 20.0% (w/w) Benzocaine (oral liquid anesthetic with brush) CVS brand www.cvs.com

Dry Mouth - Biotene Mouthwash

Bleeding gums or Gingivitis which is caused by inflammation, flossing daily – I usually do this at night while talking to a friend on speaker phone.

Toothache
Toothache Pain Relief Crème 20.0% Benzocaine
(May need to use a Q-Tip)
CVS brand
www.cvs.com

Clove Essential Oil – for dental pain, also flu & colds, acts as an anesthetic.
www.youngliving.com

Peppermint Essential Oil - relieving bad breath
www.youngliving.com

Female ZONE
Feminine Topical Analgesic/Anesthetic (if you shave or wax)
Bikini Zone Medicated Crème
2.00% Lidocaine
www.bikinizone.com

Vaginal irritation
Vagisil – Anti-itch Crème & wipes – 20.0% Benzocaine & 3% Resocrinal

Vanilla Essential Oil – Aroma & Considered a sensual aphrodisiac
www.youngliving.com

Aromatherapy always calms me. I'm an incense and candles kind of girl, and you can also use essential oils, like vanilla mmmm.

Personal Lubricant
Wet® Water based formulas – Less silicon, glycerin and paraben free.
www.stayswetlonger.com

Beauty

Molivera Organics 100% Pure Sweet Almond Oil, Cold Pressed (Also great for hair, skin, nails, and scalp). www.moliveralifeproducts.com

Makeup - Foundations, concealers that include SPF, that are hypoallergenic and natural.

Pedicure, Manicure (I am unaware that nail polish has affected me, but use the UV light as less as possible).

Eyebrows, Threading is the best because there are no chemicals involved, unless you can get a natural wax.

If you get lashes, make sure they use hypoallergenic adhesive.

Muscle Pain & Stiffness/ Arthritis
Bath Soak with Epsom Salt with Magnesium
Lavender Bath Salts

Coconut oil Bath
1/3 cup of coconut oil
10 lavender oil drops

1 cup of Epsom salt with magnesium

Essential Lotion - Two Old Goats – Arthritis & Fibromyalgia

Vicks VapoRub – (or natural ointment –camphor, eucalyptus for menthol)
www.Vicks.com

Icy Hot – Topical pain relieving cream
www.icyhot.com

Massage
Getting a lymphatic massage
Unscented free-up Professional Massage Cream for Tissue Perception and Lubricity
www.prepakproducts.com

Acupuncture
Acupuncture treatment alleviates the pain and suffering associated with Lupus, it targets organs that are weakened by emotional stress, over strain, inadequate sleep, and poor diet.

Working out and sweating seems to keep Lupus away. Try light weights and water aerobics

I keep a few wrist and knee braces around.

Be sure to take a Bone Density Test.

***REDUCE INFLAMMATION

Anti-inflammatories, your #1 BFF
Turmeric (Drops, grounded powder)

Turmeric daily use in food as a seasoning or in drinks such as tea or milk.

Turmeric Milk
Add 1 tsp. turmeric powder to 1 cup of almond milk and boil it. Sweeten with a raw honey to taste.

Yucca
Drops, Root plant (like a potato)

Digestive Health
Leaky gut, bloated, constipation – A great smoothie or your plate should resemble a Rainbow. Eat lots of greens!

Beverages
Green Tea
Apple Cider Vinegar (a shot)
Lemon water (drink lots and lots of water)
Liquid Chlorophyll it builds red bloods cells, make sure to use alcohol free

Whole grain carbohydrates are essential fiber to the Lupus intake to give you energy and always opt for gluten-free products (if you can).

Raw vegetables are a great snack
One of my fav's is carrots and hummus with spinach and artichoke.

Omega-3 fatty acids are a must!
Fish, nuts and flaxseeds are an excellent source of omega 3's because it mitigates inflammation, boosts your mood and improves your cardiovascular health.

Vitamin D and calcium for bone health.
Probiotics supplement or Greek yogurt

Spirulina is a super food and antioxidant, you can add to your drinks

I also tend to eat for my blood type as well.

I recommend downloading Dr. Sebi's Nutritional Guide and research and get familiar with the Acidic/ Alkaline food chart and what's best for you and your PH balance:

www.drsebiscellfood.com

***Avoid

Alcohol consumption
Combining alcohol with corticosteroids, Tylenol, warfarin can be harmful to the liver and stomach, so drink in moderation.

When taking methotrexate consuming alcohol is never allowed.

Alfalfa sprouts it contains an amino acid called L-canavanine that increases inflammation by stimulating the immune system.

Echinacea also boosts the immune system, which can cause a flare.

Garlic contains allicin, ajoene and thiosulfinates that boosts the immune system which is not good for those with Lupus because of the overactive immune system. I have also notice this only with whole garlic. (When in powder form it has not affected me).

Nightshade vegetables - due to the high levels of alkaloids, which appear to worsen inflammation in some people.

Eg. Potatoes, eggplant, peppers (sweet & hot), and tomatoes. Tobacco is also a member of the nightshade family.

And be very careful with birth control contraceptives with high estrogen.

If you have any questions regarding any of the suggestions please feel free to reach me on my website at

www.aleatheadijon.com.

"Once a butterfly, you cannot get back into the cocoon."
-Aleathea Díjon

Endnotes

Health Journo. (2016). WorldLupusDay: Lupus – when your body suddenly starts attacking its health cells (what you can do). Retrieved from http://www.healthjourno.com/2016/05/worldLupusda y-Lupus-when-your- body.html

Illness and Disabilities: Lupus. (2009). Retrieved from http://www.womenshealth.gov/illnesses-disabilities/types-illnesses-disabilities/lupus.html

Lupus Foundation of America, Inc.. (2017). Retrieved from http://www.lupus.org/

Maroon, Joseph C., & Bost, Jeffrey. (2006). Fish Oil: The Natural Anti-inflammatory . Laguna Beach, CA: Basic Health Publications, Inc.

(2014). In Mosby's Pocket Dictionary of Medicine, Nursing & Health Professions (7th ed.). St. Louis, MO: Elsevier Inc.

(2013). In New World Translation of the Holy Scriptures (Rev.). Walkill, NY: Watchtower Bible and Tract Society of New York, Inc.

Pasquale, Maris. (2008). The Emotional Impact of the Pain Experience: Adapted from a presentation at the SLE Workshop at Hospital for Special Surgery. Retrieved from https://www.hss.edu/conditions_emotional-impact-pain-experience.asp

Rhines, Karin. (2012). Lupus. USA TODAY health reports: diseases and disorders. Minneapolis, MN: Twenty-First Century Books.

Scott, E. (2016). Music and Stress Relief: How to Use Music In Your Daily Life. Retrieved from https://www.verywell.com/how-to-use-music-for-stress-relief-3144689

Wallace, Daniel. J. (2005). The Lupus Book: A Guide for Patients and Their Families (3rd ed.). New York, New York: Oxford University Press.

Personalized Safety Plan. (2015). Retrieved from http://www.domesticviolence.org/personalized-safety-plan/

Image credits:
Emotions and the Chronic Pain Cycle
https://www.hss.edu/conditions_emotional-impact-pain-experience.asp

The Impact of Lupus on the Body
www.lupussupportgroupni.co.uk

Stephen Covey's Urgent/Important Quadrant for time management matrix
https://www.pinterest.com/pin/125819383309528229/
(Stephen R. Covey 1994 book The 7 Habits of Highly Effective People)

Power and Control (Violence) Wheel
http://www.domesticviolence.org/violence-wheel/
Origin: www.theduluthmodel.org

Glossary

Systemic Lupus Erythematosus (SLE) Breakdown
Systemic – *pertaining to system(s)*
Lupus means wolf in Latin, and is attributed to the thirteenth century physician Rogerius, who used it to describe erosive facial lesions that were reminiscent of a wolf's bite.
Erythros – *redness or to become red in Greek*
Osis – *disease, morbid state*

acute cutaneous: a disease pertaining to the skin.

alopecia: partial or complete lack of hair resulting from normal aging, endocrine disorder, drug reaction, or skin disease.

anemia: a decrease in quality hemoglobin in the blood to levels below normal range. Anemia may be caused by a decrease in erythrocyte production, an increase in erythrocyte destruction, or a loss of blood.

antibodies: chemicals made by the immune system that bind with foreign invaders to reduce their harm to the body.

antibody-antigen complex: the combination of a foreign invader (antigen) and attached antibodies that mark invader for destruction by macrophages and other cells.

anti-depressant: pertaining to a substance or a measure that prevents or relieves depression.

anti-double stranded DNA antibody: an antibody found in about half of people with lupus that can help diagnosis.

antigen: something that invades the body and has the potential to cause illness.

antimalarials: medications originally developed to treat malaria that are effective in treating lupus cases that do not involve internal organs.

eg. Plaquenil (hydroxychloroquine)

antinuclear antibody (ANA): an antibody present in about 95% of people with lupus that is used in diagnosis.

anxiety: anticipation of impending danger and dread accompanied by restlessness, tension, tachycardia, and breathing difficulty not necessarily associated with an apparent stimulus.

arrhythmia: abnormal heart rhythm that relates to the electric control of the heart-beat. Arrhythmia can range in severity from minor to very serious; in some cases it can lead to death.

arthritis: inflammation of the joints includes pain, swelling, redness and tenderness.

autoantibodies: chemicals made by the immune system that attack the body.

autoimmune disease: a medical condition in which the immune system attacks its own body.

b cells: cells of the immune system that produce antibodies.

blood: the liquid pumped by the heart through all the arteries, vein, and capillaries. The blood is composed of a yellow fluid, called plasma, red cells, white cells, and platelets. The major function of the blood is to carry oxygen and nutrients to the cells and to remove carbon dioxide and waste products.

cardiologist: a physician who specializes in the diagnosis and treatment of disorders of the heart.

central nervous system (CNS): one of the two main divisions of the nervous system, consisting of the brain and the spinal cord. The CNS processes information to and from the peripheral nervous system and the main network of coordination and control of the entire body.

chest pain: any physical complaint that requires immediate diagnosis and evaluation.

chronic disease: an illness that lasts for a long time – sometimes a lifetime – or occurs repeatedly over time.

clinical trial: an organized study to provide large bodies of clinical data for statistically valid evaluation of treatment to determine safety and efficacy.

cognitive therapy: any of the various methods of treating mental and emotional disorders that helps a person change attitudes, perceptions, and patterns of thinking.

complete blood count (CBC): a group of blood tests that provide information on blood cells. The CBC helps doctors monitor lupus.

connective tissue: tissue that supports and binds other body tissue and parts.

corticosteroid: hormones produces in the adrenal glands. Doctors use synthetic versions of these hormones to treat moderate and severe lupus.

eg. Prednisone

costochondritis: an inflammation of the costal cartilage of the anterior chest wall, characterized by pain and tenderness.

c-reactive protein: a protein not normally found at high levels in the blood of healthy people; when present, it indicates inflammation in the body.

cytokine: a molecule that controls reactions among cells; key component of inflammation.

deoxyribonucleic acid (DNA): a large, double-stranded, helical molecule that is the carrier of genetic information. Genetic information is coded in the sequence of the nucleotides.

depression: pertaining to an emotional condition, characterized by emotional dejection, loss of initiative, listlessness, loss of appetite, and concentration difficulty.

dermatologist: a physician specializing in the skin and its properties of health and disease.

dialysis: a medical treatment for end-stage kidney disease in which the blood is filtered outside the body to remove waste and then is returned to the body.

discoid lupus (DLE): a type of lupus that affects only the skin. It produces raised, coin-shaped (discoid) rashes that can result in scarring.

disease-modifying antirheumatic drug (DMARD): a classification of antirheumatic agents referring to their ability to modify the course of disease, as opposed to simply treating symptoms.

eg. Cytoxan - used in cancer patients as chemotherapy as well as in lupus patients. Methotrexate - used in cancer patients as chemotherapy as well as in rheumatoid arthritis patients.

dry eye syndrome: a dryness of the cornea and conjunctiva caused by a deficiency in tear production or altered tear film composition

eg. Sjögren's Syndrome

edema: swelling caused by excessive accumulation of fluid in body tissues.

electrocardiogram (ECG, EKG) system: a system that that provides a graphic record produced by a device used for recording the electrical activity of the myocardium to detect specific cardiac abnormalities.

erythema: refers to redness of the skin that result from capillary congestion. Erythema can occur with inflammation, as in sunburn and allergic reactions to drugs.

fatigue: a state of exhaustion or a loss of strength or endurance.

fever: an elevation of the body temperature above normal range. Fever results from an imbalance between the elimination and the production of heat (also a sign of infection).

flare: an increase of disease activity.

gastroesophageal reflux disease (GERD): a backflow of contents of the stomach into the esophagus that is often the result of incompetence of the lower esophageal sphincter. Gastric juices are acidic and therefore produce burning pain in the esophagus.

hematologist: a medical specialist in the field of blood and blood-forming tissues.

hemoglobin: a complex protein-iron compound in the blood that carries oxygen to the cells from the lungs and carbon dioxide away from the cells to the lungs.

hidradenitis suppurativa: a chronic suppurative and cicatricial disease of the apocrine gland-bearing areas caused by occlusion of the pores with secondary bacterial infection of apocrine sweat glands.

hormone: a chemical produced by the body that acts to regulate processes within the body.

hypothyroidism: a condition characterized by decreased activity of the thyroid gland. Manifestations include weight gain, cold, pale, dry, rough hands and feet; reduced attention span with memory impairment, slowed speech, and loss of initiative; swelling in the extremities and around the eyes, eyelids, and face; menstrual irregularities; muscle aches and weakness; joint aches and stiffness; clumsiness; hyper stiff reflexes; decreased pulse; decreased BP; agitation; depression; and paranoia.

immune system: the bodies systems for protection against infection and disease; involves immune cells, antibodies, and other molecules. The principal components of the immune system include bone marrow, the thymus, and the lymphoid tissues.

immunosuppressant: group of powerful medications that "turn down" the immune system. Drugs in this group are used to treat cancer, some autoimmune diseases such as lupus and to prevent rejection of organ transplants.

infection (bacterial, viral): invasions of the body by harmful microorganisms such as viruses, bacteria, fungi, or parasites.

inflammation: the body's immediate, defensive reaction to any injury. Redness, swelling, and heat that result from the response of the immune system to an antigen.

insomnia: chronic inability to sleep or to remain asleep throughout the night; wakefulness; sleeplessness.

intravenous therapy (IV): an administration of fluids into a vein through a needle or small-caliber catheter.

kidneys: a pair of bean-shaped urinary organs located on each side of the vertebral column between the twelfth thoracic and third lumbar vertebrae. The kidneys filter the blood and eliminate wastes in the urine through a complex filtration network and resorption system.

lesions: a wound, injury, or pathologic change in body tissue. Any visible, local abnormality of the tissues of the skin, such as a wound, sore, rash, or boil.

lupus fog: is a general name for the cognitive impairments and the forgetfulness and fuzzy-headed feeling, including concentration and memory problems and are often worse during a flare.

lymphatic massage: also called a lymphatic drainage is a type of gentle massage which is intended to encourage the natural drainage of the lymph fluid, which carries waste products away from the tissues back toward the heart.

lymphatic system: a vast, complex network of capillaries, thin vessels, valves, ducts, nodes, and organs that helps protect and maintain the internal fluid environment of the entire body by producing, filtering, and conveying lymph and producing various blood cells.

macrophages: a cell of the immune system that attacks and eats foreign invaders. It also acts as a garbage collector, cleaning up debris.

malaise: a general feeling of discomfort, illness, or uneasiness

malar rash (butterfly rash): an erythematous eruption or rash that covers the cheeks and connects over the bridge of the nose.
medical noncompliance: not following doctor's advice.

mood disorder: a variety of conditions characterized by a disturbance in mood as the main feature. Other mood disorders may be caused by a general medical condition.

mood face: a condition characterized by a round ,puffy face. It occurs in people treated with large doses of corticosteroids. The features return to normal when the medication is stopped.

neurologist: a specialist that deals with the nervous system and its disorders.

nocturia: frequent and excessive urination at night.

non-steroidal anti-inflammatory drugs (NSAIDs): a group of medications that reduce inflammation. Patients often use them to treat mild to moderate lupus symptoms of the joints.

ophthalmologist: a physician that specializes in the physiology, anatomy, and pathology of the eye and the diagnosis and treatment of disorders of the eye.

osteoarthritis: a form of arthritis in which one or many joints undergo degenerative changes.

overactive bladder (OAB): is a chronic condition of the bladder that causes sudden urges to urinate. The urge comes from bladder muscle contractions. The urge can happen suddenly and at any time, regardless of the amount of urine in the bladder. It may cause urine leakage (incontinence).

overlap syndrome: the term overlap syndrome includes a large group of conditions characterized by the coexistence of signs, symptoms and immunological features of 2 or more connective tissue diseases and occurring simultaneously in the same patient.

pathogen: microorganism that causes disease.

pericarditis: inflammation of the pericardium.

pericardium: a fibro-serous sac that surrounds the heart and the roots of the great vessels.

phagocyte: any cell that ingests and destroys antigens.

photosensitivity: an abnormal reaction to sunlight and other forms of light such as ultraviolet rays, which also affect the eyes and skin.

placebo: an inactive substance, such as saline solution, distilled water, or sugar, or a less than effective dose of a harmless substance, such as a water-soluble vitamin, prescribed as if it were an effective dose of a needed medication. Placebos are used in experimental drug studies to compare the effects of the inactive substance with those of the experimental drug.

platelet: blood cells that help blood clot.

pleurisy (pleuritis): inflammation of the membranes around the lungs.

pneumonia: an acute inflammation of the lungs, often caused by inhaled pneumococci of the species Streptococcus pneumoniade. The alveoli and bronchioles of the lung become plugged with a fibrous exudate. Pneumonia may be caused by other bacteria, as well as by viruses, rickettsia, and fungi.

raynaud's phenomenon: a condition in which fingertips, toes, ears, and the tips of the nose become numb when exposed to cold, usually turning pale or blue.

red blood bell (erythrocytes): a cell that contains hemoglobin and can carry oxygen to the body. Also called a red blood cell (RBC). The reddish color is due to the hemoglobin. Erythrocytes are biconcave in shape, which increases the cell's surface area and facilitates the diffusion of oxygen and carbon dioxide.

remission: a period during which symptoms of a disease lessen or temporarily disappear.

rheumatoid arthritis (RA): an autoimmune disease that can cause permanent, crippling damage to the joints.

rheumatoid factor (RF): anti-globulin antibodies often found in the serum of patients with a clinical diagnosis of rheumatoid arthritis.

rheumatologist: a specialist in the treatment of disorders of the connective tissue.

seizure: a hyperexcitation of neurons in the braid leading to abnormal electric activity that causes a sudden, violent involuntary series of contractions of a group of muscles.

serositis: refers to inflammation of the serous tissues
of the body, the tissues lining the lungs (pleura), heart (pericardium), and the inner lining of the abdomen (peritoneum) and organs within.

sinus tachycardia: a rapid heartbeat generated by discharge of the sinus node.

sjögren's syndrome: [named after Swedish ophthalmologist Henrik S. C. Sjögren, 1899-1986] – an immunologic disorder characterized by deficient fluid production by the lacrimal, salivary, and other glands, resulting in abnormal dryness of the mouth, eyes, and other mucous membranes.

speckled pattern: an immunofluorescence pattern produced when serum from a patient with a particular connective tissue disease is placed in contact with human epithelial cells and stained with fluorochrome-labeled animal antisera.

stem cells: cells of the body capable of developing into many types of cells. Stem cells in the bone marrow give rise to all the different types of blood cells.

stress: any emotional, physical, social, economic, or other factor that requires a response or change. Stress can be positive or negative. Ongoing chronic stress can result in physical illness. Stress may also be applied therapeutically to promote change.

syndrome: a group of symptoms that occur together in a specific disease.

systemic lupus erythematosus: a chronic inflammatory disease affecting many systems of the body.

systemic inflammation: inflammation throughout the body.

tendinitis: inflammation of a tendon.

thrombocytopenia: a platelet count below the lower limit of the reference interval, usually 150,000/uL. It may be the consequence of decreased production disorders.

thrombosis: an abnormal condition in which a clot develops within a blood vessel.

transplant: a body organ or part of a body organ from one person to another. In, lupus, kidney transplants can be used to treat end-stage kidney disease.

tremors: an unintentional, rhythmic muscle movement, which can result in falling episodes involving to-and-fro movements of one or more parts of the body.

ulcer: a circumscribed, craterlike lesion of the skin or mucous membrane resulting from necrosis that accompanies some inflammatory, infectious, or malignant processes. An ulcer may be shallow, involving only the epidermis, or deep.

urinalysis: a physical, microscopic, or chemical examination of urine. Chemical analysis may be performed to measure the pH and to identify and measure the levels of ketones, sugars, protein, blood components, and many other substances.

vitamin deficiency: a state or condition resulting from the lack of or inability to use one or more vitamins. The symptoms and manifestations of each deficiency vary, depending on the specific function of the vitamin in promoting growth and development and maintaining body health.

eg. Such as Vitamin D - which you natural get from the sun, but patients diagnosed are highly recommended to stay away out of the sun, so you may develop a vitamin D deficiency.

white blood cell (leukocytes): a blood cell that participates in immunity and inflammation and is an important component in the blood system and essential for good health and protection against illness and disease. There are five categories of leukocytes.

Resources

Addiction Treatment Helpline
www.americanaddictioncenters.org
1-877-751-5859
Provides 24/7, free and confidential support.

Alliance for Lupus Research
www.lupusresearch.org
 1-800-867-1743
American   Autoimmune   Related   Diseases
Association, Inc.
 www.aarda.org
 1-586-776-3900

American Chronic Pain Association
www.theacpa.org
1-800-533-3231

American College of Rheumatology
www.rheumatology.org
1-404-633-3777

American Heart Association
www.heart.org
1-800-242-8721

American Music Therapy Association
www.musictherapy.org
1-301-589-3300
Arthritis Foundation
www.arthritis.org
1-404-872-7100

For updates and questions about statistics, please
contact:
Centers   for   Disease   Control   and   Prevention,
National Center for Health Statistics

www.cdc.gov/nchs
1-800-232-4636

Domestic Abuse Intervention Programs
www.theduluthmodel.org
1-218-722-2787

Greta Lewis Lupus Foundation (GLLF)
www.glewislupusfoundation.org
1-404-573-7248

Lupus Clinical Trials
www.Lupustrials.org
1-877-95-87425

Lupus Foundation of America
www.Lupus.org
1-202-349-1155

Lupus Foundation of America - GA Chapter
www.Lupus.org/georgia
1-770-333-5930
National Domestic Violence Hotline
1-800-799-SAFE (7233)
www.thehotline.org
Provides 24/7, free and confidential support.

If you are in any danger, please use a safe computer, or call 911 or local hotline

National Institute of Arthritis and Musculoskeletal and Skin Diseases (NIAMS) National Institutes of Health
http://www.niams.nih.gov
1-301-495-4484

National Kidney Foundation
www.kidney.org
1-800-622-9010

National Suicide Prevention Lifeline
1-800-273-TALK (8255)
www.Suicidepreventionlifeline.org
Provides 24/7, free and confidential support.

Sjögren's Syndrome Foundation
www.sjogrens.org
1-800-475-6473

SLE Lupus Foundation
www.Lupusny.org
1-212-685-4118

U.S. Food and Drug Administration
www.fda.gov
1-888-INFO-FDA (463-6332)

Additional websites

www.dometicviolence.org

www.goodtherapy.org

www.lupusmatters.org

www.mollysfund.org

www.womenshealth.gov

www.aleatheadijon.com

A subdivision under the non-profit organization, Greta Lewis Lupus Foundation to help those that have been diagnosed with Lupus with resources, education and practical support.

For speaking engagements and media please contact info@aleatheadijon.com